SECRET AGENT

JACK STALWART

The Deadly
Race to Space:
RUSSIA

BOOK ⑨

Join Agent Jack Stalwart on His Adventures:

The Search for the Sunken Treasure: **AUSTRALIA**

The Secret of the Sacred Temple: **CAMBODIA**

The Escape of the Deadly Dinosaur: **USA**

The Puzzle of the Missing Panda: **CHINA**

The Mystery of the Mona Lisa: **FRANCE**

The Caper of the Crown Jewels: **ENGLAND**

Peril at the Grand Prix: **ITALY**

The Pursuit of the Ivory Poachers: **KENYA**

The Deadly Race to Space: **RUSSIA**

The Quest for Aztec Gold: **MEXICO**

The Theft of the Samurai Sword: **JAPAN**

The Fight for the Frozen Land: **ARCTIC**

The Hunt for the Yeti Skull: **NEPAL**

The Mission to Find Max: **EGYPT**

The Deadly
Race to Space:
RUSSIA

Elizabeth Singer Hunt

Illustrated by Brian Williamson

WEINSTEIN BOOKS

For GG, who now sleeps with the stars

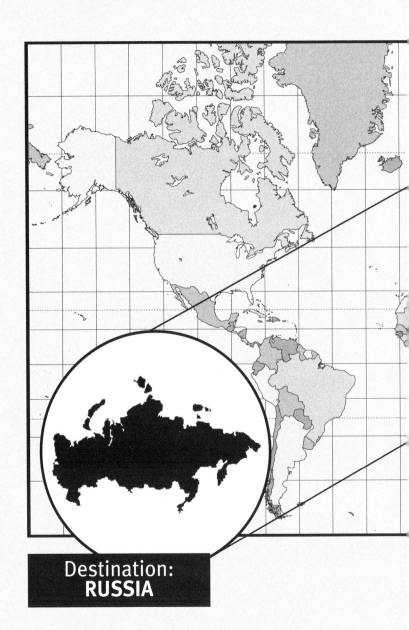

Destination:
RUSSIA

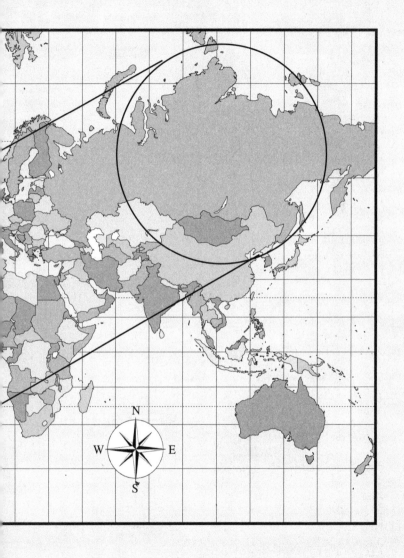

JACK STALWART

Jack Stalwart applied to be a secret
agent for the Global Protection
Force four months ago.

My name is Jack Stalwart. My older brother,
Max, was a secret agent for you, until he
disappeared on one of your missions. Now I
want to be a secret agent too. If you choose
me, I will be an excellent secret agent and get
rid of evil villains, just like my brother did.
Sincerely,

Jack Stalwart

HIGHLY CONFIDENTIAL

Jack Stalwart was sworn in as a Global Protection Force secret agent four months ago. Since that time, he has completed all of his missions successfully and has stopped no less than twelve evil villains. Because of this he has been assigned the code name "COURAGE".

Jack has yet to uncover the whereabouts of his brother, Max, who is still working for this organization at a secret location. Do not give Secret Agent Jack Stalwart this information. He is never to know about his brother.

Gerald Barter
Director, Global Protection Force

THINGS YOU'LL FIND IN EVERY BOOK

Watch Phone: The only gadget Jack wears all the time, even when he's not on official business. His Watch Phone is the central gadget that makes most others work. There are lots of important features, most importantly the "C" button, which reveals the code of the day—necessary to unlock Jack's Secret Agent Book Bag. There are buttons on both sides, one of which ejects his life-saving Melting Ink Pen. Beyond these functions, it also works as a phone and, of course, gives Jack the time of day.

Global Protection Force (GPF): The GPF is the organization Jack works for. It's a worldwide force of young secret agents whose aim is to protect the world's people, places and possessions. No one knows exactly where its main offices are located (all correspondence and gadgets for repair are sent to a special PO Box, and training is held at various locations around the world), but Jack thinks it's somewhere cold, like the Arctic Circle.

Whizzy: Jack's magical miniature globe. Almost every night at precisely 7:30 P.M., the GPF uses Whizzy to send Jack the identity of the country that he must travel to. Whizzy can't talk, but he can cough up messages. Jack's parents don't know Whizzy is anything more than a normal globe.

The Magic Map: The magical map hanging on Jack's bedroom wall. Unlike most maps, the GPF's map is made of a mysterious wood. Once Jack inserts the country piece from Whizzy, the map swallows Jack whole and sends him away on his missions. When he returns, he arrives precisely one minute after he left.

Secret Agent Book Bag: The Book Bag that Jack wears on every adventure. Licensed only to GPF secret agents, it contains top-secret gadgets necessary to foil bad guys and escape certain death. To activate the bag before each mission, Jack must punch in a secret code given to him by his Watch Phone. Once he's away, all he has to do is place his finger on the zip, which identifies him as the owner of the bag and immediately opens.

THE STALWART FAMILY

Jack's dad, John

He moved the family to England when Jack was two, in order to take a job with an aerospace company. Jack's dad thinks he is an ordinary boy and that his other son, Max, attends a school in Switzerland. Jack's dad is American and his mum is British, which makes Jack a bit of both.

Jack's mum, Corinne

One of the greatest mums as far as Jack is concerned. When she and her husband received a letter from a posh school in Switzerland inviting Max to attend, they were overjoyed. Since Max left six months ago, they have received numerous notes in Max's handwriting telling them he's OK. Little do they know it's all a lie and that it's the GPF sending those letters.

Jack's older brother, Max

Two years ago, at the age of nine, Max joined the GPF. Max used to tell Jack about his adventures and show him how to work his secret-agent gadgets. When the family received a letter inviting Max to attend a school in Europe, Jack figured it was to do with the GPF. Max told him he was right, but that he couldn't tell Jack anything about why he was going away.

Nine-year-old Jack Stalwart

Four months ago, Jack received an anonymous note saying: "Your brother is in danger. Only you can save him." As soon as he could, Jack applied to be a secret agent too. Since that time, he's battled some of the world's most dangerous villains, and hopes some day in his travels to find and rescue his brother, Max.

DESTINATION:
Russia

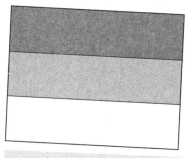

The main language of Russia is Russian. It is based on a 33-letter alphabet called the Cyrillic alphabet.

❏

Russia's currency is the Ruble.

❏

The first man in space was a Russian named Yuri Gagarin. Today Russia operates the world's oldest and largest space launch facility, the Baikonur Cosmodrome.

Russia is the largest country on the planet. It stretches from northeast Europe across to northern Asia.

❏

Its proper name is the Russian Federation.

❏

Moscow is Russia's capital city and the largest city in Europe. 11 million people live there.

SPACE CRAFTS: FACTS AND FIGURES

In 1957, the Russians sent the first ever space craft, called *Sputnik 1*, into space.

Space rockets are usually made of several sections. The bottom sections carry the fuel and the top sections carry the astronauts.

When the bottom sections of fuel are used up, they usually fall off. Kerosene and liquid hydrogen are typically used to fuel the rocket.

A rocket needs to travel at 25,250 miles per hour (40,635 km/h) to escape Earth's gravity and at least 17,500 mph (28,165 km/h) to keep it circling around Earth.

THE SOLAR SYSTEM

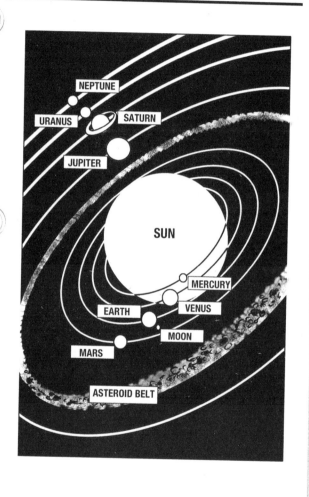

MARS: FACTS AND FIGURES

Mars is called the "red planet." It got its name from the Romans, who named it after the god of war. (Red reminded them of blood).

It's the closest planet to Earth in the Solar System— only 300 million miles (480 million km) away.

The surface of Mars is dry and dusty, with lots of rocks and craters. One of the largest craters is 200 miles (320 km) across and thousands of miles long.

Mars has a North and South Pole that are covered by ice and frozen carbon dioxide. Temperatures at the poles can drop to as low as −115°C.

Mars used to have running water. Scientists have seen pictures that show riverbeds and flat areas that could have been oceans.

Gravity on Mars is only ⅓ of Earth's. If you weighed 40 kilograms (90 pounds) on Earth, you'd only weigh 13.34 kilograms (30 pounds) on Mars.

RUSSIAN ALPHABET

А а (A)	Р р (R)
Б б (B)	С с (S)
В в (V)	Т т (T)
Г г (G)	У у (U)
Д д (D)	Ф ф (F)
Е е (E)	Х х (KH)
Ё ё (YO)	Ц ц (TS)
Ж ж (ZH)	Ч ч (CH)
З з (Z)	Ш ш (SH)
И и (I)	Щ щ (SHCH)
Й й (Y)	ъ (–)
К к (K)	ы (Y)
Л л (L)	ь (')
М м (M)	Э э (E)
Н н (N)	Ю ю (YU or IU)
О о (O)	Я я (YA or IA)
П п (P)	

SECRET AGENT PHRASEBOOK FOR RUSSIA

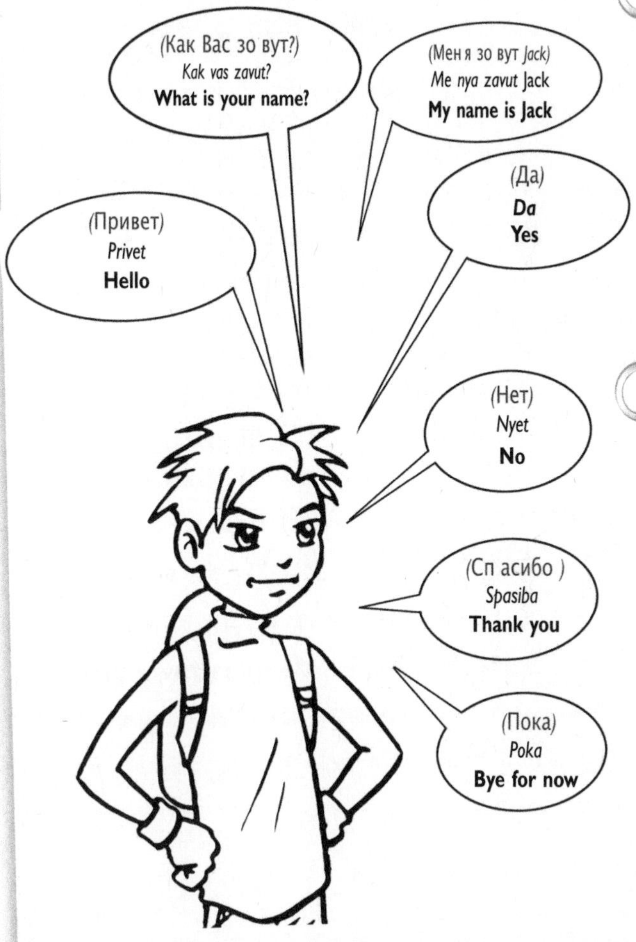

SECRET AGENT GADGET INSTRUCTION MANUAL

Smoke-Screen Pellets: When you need to distract someone or something, use the GPF's Smoke-Screen Pellets. These sticky blue pellets emit smoke so thick it's impossible to see anything through it for two minutes. Just throw them at your target—they activate on impact.

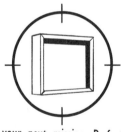

Portable Map: Small enough to fit in your Book Bag, this wooden square opens up to the size of your Magic Map. Just place the jigsaw piece inside as normal and it will transport you to your next mission. Perfect when you're traveling and away from home.

Mind Eraser: When you need to erase somebody's short-term memory, hand them the GPF's Mind Eraser. Just flick the switch on this rectangular box and tell them to stare at the swirling spirals inside. After a few minutes, they'll forget what happened in the last 48 hours.

Gripper Gloves: If you need a little extra grip, slip on a pair of Gripper Gloves. These gloves have a special grip fabric that prevents you from slipping, even on the smoothest of materials. Great for climbing shiny poles, steel columns or any outdoor structure.

Chapter 1:
The Night Sky

It was a clear, dark night, and Jack
Stalwart was lying on his back gazing at
the stars. He was with his local Scouts
group on a camping trip in the New Forest
in England. As part of the activities, his
troop leader had told Jack and the other
boys to observe the night sky, try to spot
the constellations and think about the
possibility of life beyond planet Earth.

"Do you see that star over there?" asked Jack's friend Richard, pointing to a brilliant white light. "It's not a star," he said, "but the International Space Station—the brightest light in the night sky."

Jack knew that Richard was right. The International Space Station—also known as the ISS—was a man-made satellite that orbited 220 miles, or 354 kilometers, above Earth. It was the biggest laboratory in the sky, where scientists carried out research on everything from cancer to how plants grow and the effects of living in space.

Astronauts were constantly being ferried to and from the ISS. It took them about two days to get there. Once they were there, they could stay for months, and the longest any astronaut had lived on the station was two years. Jack knew a lot about the ISS because the GPF received daily "live" updates.

The GPF, or Global Protection Force, was the organization that Jack worked for. He was a secret agent for them, traveling the globe to protect the world's most precious treasures. But no one knew anything about that—not even his family or his best friends.

Richard and Jack continued staring at all the stars. Their other friend, Charlie, was lying beside them, making a note of the constellations they could see, like Orion.

"I can't believe we're finally going to send a human to Mars," said Jack. He stretched out his arms, placed his hands behind his head and thought about how amazing it was.

Tomorrow's Mars mission was all over the news. After decades of planning, a team of Americans and Russians were sending six astronauts—three men and three women—to the red planet.

It would take more than a year to complete the journey, but it didn't matter how long it took. Sending a human to Mars was one of the biggest things in space history—as important as when the American astronaut Neil Armstrong walked on the moon.

"I know," said Charlie. "It's incredible. I wonder what the astronauts are doing right now."

"Did you know," said Jack, "that my dad's going to be there? He's going to see the rocket liftoff up close." Jack couldn't help but brag about his dad, who was an aerospace engineer. During his career, he'd helped design some American spy

satellites, and parts of the International Space Station.

Since moving to England, Jack's father only worked on special projects. A few years ago he'd been awarded the job of designing the Mars spacecraft itself. He was in Russia right now, supervising the final details before the rocket was launched.

"That's what I want to be when I'm older," said Charlie.

"An aerospace engineer?" asked Jack, still thinking about his dad.

"No, you silly," said Charlie. "An astronaut!"

"You—an astronaut?" said Richard, teasing Charlie. "You don't have what it takes!"

"Yes, I do," said Charlie. "You watch," he told them. "I'm going to be the first person to walk on Jupiter!"

Jack and Richard looked at each other and then cracked up laughing. There was no way Charlie was going to "walk" on Jupiter. Except for a tiny rock core, Jupiter was nothing but a big ball of gas.

Chapter 2:
The Portable Map

As Jack lay there imagining Charlie in
space, he heard a small beep coming
from his GPF Watch Phone. It was 7:25 P.M.,
and he had to find somewhere secure.
It didn't matter that Jack was in the
middle of Scouts, he had to be ready to
respond.

Telling his friends he needed the "restroom," Jack wandered off and found a
hidden spot behind some trees in the

forest. Reaching into the front pocket of his Book Bag, he pulled out his miniature globe, named Whizzy.

"Hi, Whizzy," said Jack, placing the magic globe in the palm of his hand.

As the clock ticked over to 7:30 P.M., Whizzy winked and began to spin. The faster he got, the more he tickled Jack's hand, until he coughed—*ahem!*—and a giant jigsaw piece popped out of his mouth.

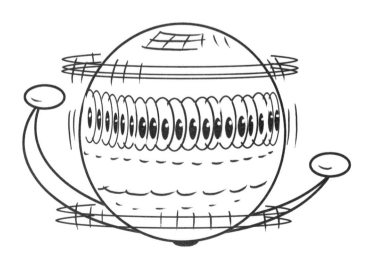

Normally, if Jack were at home, he'd slip the piece into the Magic Map, on his wall. Then he'd know the exact location of his next adventure. But for moments like this—when secret agents were away from home—the GPF had created another way to transport them to their destination.

Jack put a tired Whizzy back into the pocket of his Book Bag and keyed the letter "C" into his Watch Phone. The code word C-A-V-I-A-R appeared on the screen, and he tapped the letters into his Book Bag's lock.

As his Secret Agent Book Bag popped open, Jack looked around to make sure that no one was nearby. Inside his bag were some new gadgets: the Mind Eraser, the Noggin Mold and the SatMap device. But fitted into a side pocket was what he was looking for—a thin wooden board folded up on its hinges into a tidy square.

Jack unfolded the board until it grew to twice his size and showed a big map of the world. He laid it down on the ground, picked up the jigsaw piece and began to trace it over the map. The piece was so big it was easy to guess which country it would be. When Jack got to the top of Asia the jigsaw piece slipped in, and the name RUSSIA flashed before his eyes. Now Jack knew where he was headed, but as always, he didn't know why.

Maybe someone had stolen a priceless

Fabergé egg from a Moscow museum. Or perhaps the president of Russia was in trouble at the Kremlin. As the white light inside the country on his board began to glow, Jack stepped onto the wooden map and shut his eyes. Opening one eye quickly to make sure that no one was watching, he yelled, "Off to Russia!"

With those words and a burst of light, Jack and his portable Magic Map disappeared from the forest.

Chapter 3:
The Missing Man

As soon as Jack arrived in Russia, he
packed away his map and took a good
look around. He was at the back of a large
semicircular room filled with dozens of
people. Most were busy at work, seated
in front of computers. Others were talking
and walking around. From what Jack could
tell, they were speaking English, although
he could hear bits of Russian, French and
Italian too.

High on the wall and at the front was a giant movie screen. Every few seconds the image on the screen would change. The first was of some flatbed trucks carrying goods, and the next was of a cockpit with six seats inside. The last was of a tall, brown rocket. Suddenly Jack realized where he was, and he tried to duck out of view.

"Hello, there," said a husky voice, startling Jack.

Jack turned to his side. Standing beside him was a man wearing a gray jacket, white shirt and black tie.

"You must be Jack," he said, holding out his hand. Although he was speaking in English, the man sounded Russian.

Jack paused. He thought he recognized the man from somewhere.

"I'm Yuri," the man said. "Yuri Ivanov."

Now Jack knew who he was. Yuri was

the person in charge of the Mars mission launch. He was Jack's dad's boss.

Although Jack hadn't met him before, he'd seen pictures of Yuri in the *GPF News*—the electronic newspaper for everyone who worked for the GPF. The Mars project was so important that everyone was talking about it.

Yuri had a strong, square-shaped face. He was handsome except for the bushy white eyebrows that hung over his pale blue eyes.

"*Privet*," said Jack, respectfully shaking his hand. *Privet* was Russian for "hello." "It's a pleasure to meet you."

Yuri nodded back with a smile. Jack guessed he was pleased that he knew a bit of Russian.

"What seems to be the problem?" asked Jack, who was busily scanning the room for his dad. The last thing he needed was for his father to see him here.

"You see this?" Yuri asked, lifting his hands in the air. "This is the Mars Mission Control Center. The command center for the world's first manned mission to Mars."

"I know," said Jack. "Is there a problem with the launch?"

"Hopefully not, with your help," said Yuri. "In a few hours we are due to send the first humans to Mars. Everything is ready to go," he explained, "except for one thing."

"What's that?" asked Jack, who couldn't believe that something might be wrong.

Yuri took a deep breath. "One of our key engineers has disappeared."

Now, thought Jack, that's a problem. If something had gone wrong with one of the chief engineers, the launch to Mars would definitely be in trouble. As he listened to Yuri, he continued to look around for his dad.

Yuri carried on. "I need you to find this person and bring him back to Mission Control. Without him, we can't launch the rocket."

"Who's the missing person?" asked Jack, his eyes following a man who looked like his father from the back.

Yuri paused before answering. "John Stalwart," he said. As if Jack didn't know who that was, Yuri added, "The engineer who's vanished is your dad."

Chapter 4:
The Last Place

Jack shook his head, as if to get Yuri's voice out from between his ears. He couldn't believe what he was hearing.

"What do you mean?" he said. "My dad can't be missing. This is the biggest thing in his career. Maybe he's gone for a long walk or something."

"I don't think so," said Yuri. "He's been gone for quite a while."

"How long?" asked Jack, who was starting to worry.

"Since yesterday," replied Yuri.

Jack's thoughts traveled back to his home in England. The last time he and his mum had spoken to his dad was two days ago. He'd sounded excited about the project. There's no way he would just leave it behind.

"Why didn't you contact someone earlier?" asked Jack, getting annoyed that Yuri had left it so long.

"We didn't want to alarm anyone," said Yuri. "We thought that perhaps he'd taken himself off for a while—you know, to have a break. Working under conditions like this can be hard. But when he didn't come back this morning, we began to worry. That's when I decided to call the GPF."

Jack was getting nervous now. With at least one day gone, his dad could be anywhere. This wasn't good news.

"Do you think it's possible that someone took him?" asked Jack. He didn't like to think about it, but there was a possibility that his dad had been kidnapped.

"Maybe," said Yuri. "We're competing with several other space agencies," he explained, "any one of which would benefit from taking your dad. He knows things that other engineers don't. After all, he was the main designer of the Mars spacecraft itself. Plus, he's the only one with the code."

"What code?" asked Jack.

"The code that begins the countdown," said Yuri. "The ten-second countdown to launch can only be activated by entering a special code. And your dad," he added, "is the only one who knows it."

Although Jack was worried about his dad, he couldn't help but be impressed. To be the only one with the code that launched one of the biggest and most famous space rockets in history was a pretty cool job.

"Where was he last seen?" asked Jack.

The Russian man pointed to a sign sticking up in the middle of the room. "He was sitting at his desk in the middle of Quadrant Three," said Yuri.

On the desk were letters that looked like a "T" and a "P" and a backward "N." *TPN* spells the word "three" in Russian.

Now that Jack had a starting point, he was anxious to get to work. He turned to Yuri. "Next time you see me, I'll have my dad," he promised.

"I hope so," said Yuri with a smile. "I'm counting on it."

Jack nodded a quick goodbye, and then dashed through the control center toward his dad's desk.

Chapter 5:
The Note

When Jack reached the desk, he recognized it immediately. In a big picture frame was a photo of the Stalwart family: Jack, Max and their parents. Jack remembered the day they took the photo. It was just before Max was shipped off to "school." He looked at his brother and thought about how much he missed him.

"I wish you were here," Jack said, closing his eyes and whispering to his

brother to bring him good luck. Then he put the picture back on the desk and began to look around for clues. There was no more time to lose.

Besides the family picture, his dad had some pencils, paper and rulers on his desk. As Jack looked through various things, he noticed a plain pad of paper to his right. On it was something scribbled in ink.

It said:

Maybe his dad's disappearance was related to this note, thought Jack. As he looked at the scribble, he realized there were four important clues.

Taking the Encryption Notebook from his Book Bag, Jack placed his thumb on the identification pad. When it recognized him as the owner, it switched itself on.

Looking at his Watch Phone, Jack noticed it was 5:30 A.M., Russian time. He grabbed his pen and began to take notes.

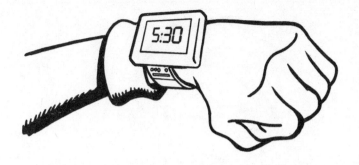

1) Not in Dad's handwriting.

2) Meeting place has three letters or words.

3) According to Yuri, he's been gone for at least one day.

4) Told to bring laptop.

Jack needed to work out who wrote this note. He pulled out his Signature ID, the only gadget in the world that could analyze someone's handwriting and tell an agent whose it was. As he scanned the device over the paper, the word CLASSIFIED popped up. Now, *that* was a surprise.

The GPF almost never classified someone's identity. Classified status was reserved for top-secret officials who the GPF believed were "free and clear" of bad behavior. Maybe whoever met Jack's dad had nothing to do with his disappearance after all.

Moving on to the next clue, Jack noticed that the location of the meeting was given as APH. Because he didn't know enough about the Mission Control complex, it was time to use the GPF's SatMap gadget.

The SatMap could display a 3-D map of any government building in the world, including its underground bunkers. It had this information thanks to pictures taken by agents on the ground and by satellites in space.

Jack typed in the related information. As the word LOADING appeared on the screen, he crossed his fingers and hoped it would provide the details he needed.

Within moments a virtual map of the Mars Mission Control Center grounds appeared on the SatMap. Jack used his finger to drag the cursor across the screen from one location to another, looking for any building with the letters APH.

There it was!

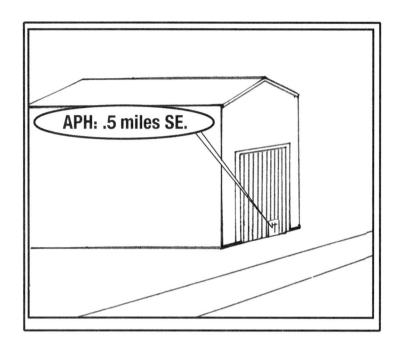

Jack tapped the screen, zooming in on the building. More information about the APH popped up.

Abandoned warehouse used for storage of faulty equipment.

That's odd, thought Jack. Why would Dad be meeting an important official in an abandoned warehouse?

Feeling uneasy, Jack locked his Book Bag and made his way toward the EXIT sign. Around him everyone was too busy at work to notice him. They didn't know that John Stalwart was missing, and that the launch they were working on was at risk.

According to the SatMap, the APH warehouse was half a mile southeast of the main building. Jack opened the doors to the outside and began to run. There was no time to waste. He had to find his dad.

Chapter 6:
The Brown Beauty

As Jack ran, he took a good look at the grounds around Mission Control. It was definitely a strange place. There were barely any people outside and the ground was dry and dusty. The only things around were concrete buildings. If Jack hadn't known they were making history inside, he would have thought the whole place was abandoned.

To his right and in the distance, Jack

spied a launchpad. He pulled his Google Goggles out of his Book Bag and flicked the switch to "maximum length". Within moments, he was gazing at the most beautiful rocket he'd ever seen. It was the Mars spacecraft itself—the very one his dad had designed. His father had shown him pictures of it before, but nothing compared to seeing it for real.

It was as tall as a skyscraper, and was painted a beautiful dark metallic brown. Russian and American flags decorated the middle, and at the top was a bright red triangular section. This was the "command module"—the cockpit where the astronauts would sit on their way into space.

Once the rocket had escaped from the Earth's gravitational pull, the command module would separate from the rest of the craft. It would take the astronauts to the ISS, where they would rest and then carry on for the orbit around Mars. Then, they would transfer to a Mars lander and make their long-awaited arrival on the red planet.

The plan was perfect, except for the fact that Jack's dad was missing and no one else knew the code to start the countdown.

Glancing back at the compass on his SatMap gadget, Jack made sure that it was pointing southeast. Then he started moving again. The APH was within reach, and hopefully, so was his dad.

Chapter 7:
The Attack

When Jack got to the building, he noticed
that it looked like an airplane hangar.
Makes sense, thought Jack, thinking of
the initials APH.

The hangar's roof was made of
corrugated iron, and the closed doors
were huge and on sliding rails. Jack put
the SatMap back into his bag as he
looked around for anyone or anything
suspicious.

Once he'd decided the outside was safe, Jack put his ear against the front doors of the building. He couldn't hear any noise inside, but just to be sure, he pulled out the GPF's Body-Count Tracker.

The Body-Count Tracker could map out walls and rooms and tell an agent if there were any people inside. It did this by showing a green or red dot. Green meant the person was alive and red meant they were dead.

According to the Body-Count Tracker, there was one steady green dot in the center of the building, and two moving green dots in the extreme left corner. Hoping that at least one of these dots was his dad, Jack carefully pulled the handle and the door slid open.

But as he stepped inside, a brilliant light flashed from the middle of the room and hit Jack's chest. It threw him

backward with such force that he fell and skidded on his backside.

As Jack lay there in the dirt, he wondered who and what had hit him. He'd heard about a criminal gadget that used the power of the sun to zap people. As he tried to pull himself up, his head started to spin. Jack had no energy. He slumped to the ground again.

The last thing Jack remembered was the sound of a man laughing and another coming toward him shouting the word "no." When he looked toward the voices, he thought he saw his dad.

"Dad," Jack called out to his father.

Then his eyes rolled backward and everything went black.

Chapter 8:
The Reason Why

When Jack came to, he was sitting in a chair with his head hanging down. His body was tired and rubbery, and a line of drool was hanging out of his mouth. He slurped it up, wiped his mouth on his shoulder, and tried to get control of his senses.

Jack didn't know how long he'd been unconscious, because he couldn't get to his Watch Phone. His wrists and chest were bound with tape behind his chair, and his feet were strapped up too. Although his Book Bag was still behind him, he couldn't reach any of his GPF gadgets, even his Melting Ink Pen.

Jack tried to remember the moment before he collapsed. What was that light that had hit him? Was that his dad running toward him? But where was he now? And who was responsible for tying Jack to the chair?

Suddenly he could hear voices. It was his dad! He was speaking to another man in a nearby room.

"Let him go," said his dad. "He's just a boy!"

"Is he?" the man replied. Jack recognized the thick Russian accent immediately. It was Yuri, and he wasn't being very nice. "Maybe you should ask him what he does in his spare time."

"What do you mean?" asked his dad. "He plays football! He does what any other ordinary boy does."

"That's what *you* think," sneered the Russian.

"What are you talking about?" asked John Stalwart.

Jack was getting worried. Was Yuri going to blow his cover? And why was he being so nasty?

"We're wasting time," said Yuri, moving on to something else. "You need to give me that launch code now."

"I told you before," said Jack's father. "I'm not going to give it to you. We need to add more water tanks and plastic shields to the rocket before I'll approve the liftoff."

Jack knew that one of the biggest dangers for astronauts flying outside of Earth's protective magnetic field was exposure to deadly galactic cosmic rays.

GCRs came from the sun and could penetrate even the thickest of metals.

They could get inside a spacecraft and damage human cells and organs, leading to death.

One of the best ways to protect the astronauts was by adding water tanks and hydrogen-based plastics to the inside walls of the spacecraft. Jack knew that his dad's original design included plenty of those, but it sounded as though he wanted to add more.

"What we have is fine!" shouted Yuri. "Adding additional tanks and plastics could take months!" he fumed. "I don't think I need to remind you that the Europeans are poised to launch their rocket too."

"I'm not giving you the code if lives are at risk," said Jack's dad. "And that's that."

"Perhaps I haven't made myself clear," said Yuri. His voice sounded evil now. "This is not for discussion. You will give me that code, or else."

"Or else what?" said John Stalwart angrily. Jack was proud that his dad didn't sound scared.

"Or else . . . your son will suffer because of you!" Yuri shouted.

Now Jack knew why he was here. He was "bait." Yuri was trying to use the threat of harming him to get to his dad. The GPF would be angry to hear that one of their agents had been called for and then used as a bargaining tool. Jack wondered if maybe this kind of trick had been used to lure and trap his missing brother, Max.

Everything went silent. There was a long pause in the conversation in the other room. Jack could almost feel his dad's anger through the walls before he suddenly let out a loud roar.

"You're not going to get away with this!" John Stalwart yelled. Jack could hear the sound of a fight. He really wanted to help his dad, but he couldn't move.

Yuri shouted something in Russian. Suddenly, the same flash of light that had hit Jack appeared from the other room.

Everything went quiet again. Then he heard a low moan. It sounded as though his dad had been zapped by the same thing.

"Westerners," he heard Yuri grunt. "We'll see *who* tells *who* what to do." Then he let out a sharp whistle. Jack heard more footsteps in the room. "Clean him up, Vigo," the Russian ordered. Then everything fell silent.

Chapter 9:
The Code

Jack sat there helplessly, trying to figure out what to do. He knew from his own experience that the light stunned rather than eliminated on impact. But he was still worried about his dad. Was he okay?

Jack heard some rustling, and then a man appeared at the door. He must be Vigo—the third green light on Jack's Body-Count Tracker and the guy Yuri had asked to "clean up" his dad.

Reaching behind him, Vigo pulled something forward and then heaved it across the floor. Jack eyes opened wide in shock when he saw that it was his father.

Vigo left for a few moments and reappeared with a chair. Placing it in front of Jack, he lifted John Stalwart's body onto it. Quickly, he taped his wrists and feet, then strapped his chest to the chair like Jack's. When he was finished, he hurried off.

Jack took a look at his dad. Except for having been knocked out, he looked fine— no cuts or wounds.

"Uhhhh," groaned his dad. Jack could see him struggle to open his eyes.

"Dad!" whispered Jack anxiously. "Are you okay?"

"I'm okay," his dad replied. His speech was slurred. "Are *you* okay?" he asked as his head rolled from side to side. "What was that light? I don't know how Yuri got

you here, but your mother must be very worried."

At the mention of his name, Yuri entered the room.

"How nice," he said with a wicked smile. "A family reunion—it warms the heart." Jack could tell from his voice that he wasn't being sincere.

"Shut it, Yuri," said Jack's dad, his eyes more focused now.

"Come now, John," said the Russian

with fake sympathy. "There's no need for that kind of reaction. Besides," he added, "you'll be happy to know that I may not need the two of you anyway."

Jack and his dad looked at Yuri.

"Remember that laptop you brought with you?" he asked, looking at Jack's dad. "Well, Alexei is about to extract the code."

Jack glanced at his dad. His normally rosy complexion was draining to a pale white.

"You see, Jack," Yuri explained, "a few days ago, your dad let slip that he'd hidden the code in a math puzzle on his computer. All I needed to do was lure him here, get his laptop, and then put my chief hacker, Alexei, on the job." The Russian man smiled to himself. "But just in case Alexei couldn't do it," he added, "I brought you here, to encourage your dad to cough up the code."

"You're mad!" screamed Jack's dad. "You'll never get away with this. You need my final approval for the launch anyway."

"You flatter yourself, John," said Yuri. "That's what I'm *supposed* to do, but I'm about to change the rules. After all, I'm the boss. I'll just tell the others that in the last few hours you've come down with a bizarre illness, and I've isolated you in the infirmary. With that little tidbit," Yuri snickered, "no one will want to come looking for you."

"You might be able to launch the rocket," said Jack's dad, "but as soon as I'm free, I'll tell the media! I'll see to it that the rocket is brought back down to Earth before any damage is done."

"You could do that, but you're assuming that I'm going to let you go," said Yuri. Then he let out an evil laugh.

Jack gulped. He knew what Yuri was planning to do . . . He was about to get rid of them both.

Just at that moment, Yuri received a phone call. He answered it in Russian. When he hung up, he smiled like a man who had just received the best news of his life.

"Alexei," he said, "has the code. That means you're not

needed anymore, John." Yuri motioned to his accomplice. "Vigo here," he explained, "is going to take you both for a ride. To a place where you'll be able to experience the power of the rocket firsthand."

As Yuri left the room, he added, "It will be the last thing either of you remembers."

Chapter 10:
The Deadly Drive

Vigo sliced through the tape around each of
their chests, and then loosened the rope
around their ankles only slightly. Yanking
them both to a standing position, he
shoved them out of the room and through
the main doors of the airplane hangar.

Once outside, Vigo directed them
toward a truck. Waddling toward it, the
Stalwarts looked like a couple of
penguins.

"If you let us go now," said Jack, trying to reason with the Russian, "we promise not to press charges."

Vigo laughed as he opened one of the truck's doors.

"Get in!" he grunted. Jack guessed he wasn't changing his mind.

Jack and his dad climbed awkwardly into the back. While Vigo got into the driver's seat, Jack quietly grabbed the door handle and tried to open it.

But it couldn't open from the inside. Vigo started the engine and drove off.

As they set off, Jack looked out of the window. There was no one in sight—nobody to signal to, or to cry to for help. He looked at his dad. Jack had never seen him look so worried.

Up ahead was the Mars spacecraft, which Vigo proceeded to drive around the back of. He pulled up alongside what looked like an electric fence and got out of the truck. He opened a padlock on the main gate and then drove through the entrance. As they passed by, Jack noticed a sign that read DANGER: RESTRICTED ACCESS ONLY.

Ignoring the warning, Vigo carried on until he found a secluded spot behind

some old scaffolding. There, he lugged
Jack and his dad out of the vehicle and
tossed them onto the tarmac. Jack could
hear his dad grunt in pain—he was still
feeling the shock from that burst of light.

Before Jack could do anything, Vigo reached down and tied their feet tightly together again. Satisfied that Jack and his dad were going nowhere fast, Vigo got back in the truck and started the engine. As he hit the accelerator, fumes from the exhaust blew into Jack's face. Coughing through the bad air, Jack watched Vigo drive in the direction of Mission Control.

From where he was lying, Jack could see the rocket's powerful boosters several hundred yards away. Knowing that anything within a mile of liftoff would be burned to a crisp, he closed his eyes and tried to think of a plan. The Stalwarts had to get out of there, and fast.

Chapter 11:
The Stalwart Idea

"Dad," said Jack, as soon as Vigo disappeared, "we have to get out of here!"

"I know," replied his dad, who was trying to sort through things in his head. "I'm working on that."

But Jack had already come up with an idea. "Look, Dad," he said, "I've got a plan. I need you to do exactly as I say."

"Wait a minute," said his dad, trying to calm Jack down. "I know you watch these ninja shows on TV. But watching them doesn't make you a ninja, okay? Stuff like this is better handled by a grown-up. You're still only nine, remember, Jack."

Jack almost wet himself laughing. If only his dad knew that he was an agent for the GPF.

"What's so funny?" asked his dad.

"Look, Dad," said Jack, "I know a few things. I can't tell you from where, but you have to trust me that I can get us free. Will you just listen to my idea at least?"

John Stalwart looked his son in the eye. "Okay," he said reluctantly. At least for the moment he seemed willing to listen.

Jack turned his back to his dad. "Right, roll over so that your back is facing mine." His dad did as he was told.

"Then try to reach the edge of the tape around my wrists," said Jack. He could feel his dad's fingers scraping along the tape, and finally he managed to grab a bit of the end.

"Now," Jack instructed, "try to peel it off." As John Stalwart pulled, Jack moved his hands up and down. As he did so, his dad was able to unravel the tape.

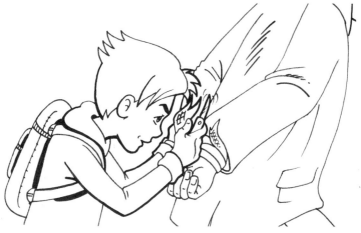

"Great!" said Jack, pushing himself into a sitting position. He reached into his Book Bag and took out his pocket knife.

Slicing through the tape around his feet, Jack was able to stand up. Rushing over to his dad, he did the same for him, cutting the tape from his hands and legs.

Jack's father looked impressed. "Well," he said, rubbing his wrists and ankles, "they've certainly taught you a few things in the Scouts!"

"Huh?" replied Jack, almost forgetting his dad didn't know about the GPF. "Oh, yeah," he said. "They've pretty much taught me everything I know." He smiled to himself.

"Well, looks like Yuri kidnapped the wrong boy, doesn't it?" said John Stalwart, laughing.

Jack really wanted to tell his dad all about the GPF, but he knew he couldn't. He decided it was safer to change the subject. "How are you feeling now? If I can get us to Mission Control, can you stop the launch?"

"I think my head is clearing now," said his dad. "Just get me to the control desk. Even if Yuri has entered the code, there's still time to hit the 'emergency shutdown' button. That's the best way to put an end to the launch."

"Terrific," said Jack. He looked at the time on his Watch Phone. It was 7:10 A.M. There were only twenty minutes left until the rocket took off.

Given the time it took Vigo to drive here, Jack reckoned they were at least five miles away from Mission Control. There was no way they could run—even the fastest runner in the world couldn't sprint it in twenty minutes. There was only one thing to do.

Reaching into his Book Bag, Jack pulled his Flyboard out. He snapped it together and laid it on the ground.

"Hop on!" said Jack to his dad, motioning for him to climb on top.

"What kind of skateboard is this?" asked his dad. Jack could tell he was confused by the fact that it didn't have wheels.

"I borrowed it from Richard," said Jack, trying to act cool. "His dad picked it up in Hong Kong while he was there on business. It's not in the shops at home yet," he added. Jack thought it best not to say anything else.

"Impressive," said his dad, stepping on. "It's amazing what toys kids have now."

"Yeah, this is a really special one. And now put this on," Jack said as he tossed a rubbery shell to his dad.

As Jack's father placed the Noggin Mold on his head, it hardened into a helmet. The Noggin Mould was great protection when you were climbing, skiing or just going fast.

Jack took the spare Noggin Mold from his Book Bag and placed it on his own

head. When he was ready, he stepped onto the Flyboard in front of his dad, and his dad grabbed hold of his shoulders.

Without his father seeing, Jack tapped a few commands into his Watch Phone. The Flyboard gently lifted and two hydrogen jets popped out from underneath. Within moments, the Stalwarts were sailing away from the rocket and toward Mission Control.

Chapter 12:
The Arrival

Once they were near the main building, Jack began to slow the Flyboard down. He turned to his dad. "Is there a back entrance to this place?" he asked.

His dad pointed to the left of the building. "On that side of the building is the delivery area," he said into Jack's ear. "Nobody will be in there now."

Slowly guiding the Flyboard to the left, Jack quieted the hydrogen jets down to a hum. He and his dad hopped off. Once the jets disappeared, Jack packed the Flyboard away.

"I hope Richard has insurance for that thing," said his dad. He was obviously impressed with how the Flyboard worked.

"I'll tell him," said Jack, who was already thinking about the next part of his plan.

"How do we get in?" he asked.

"Thumbprint identification," said his dad. He walked over and placed his thumb on a black box outside the door. "Let's hope Yuri hasn't flagged me," he said.

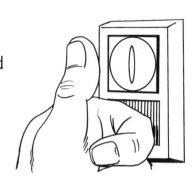

Jack knew there was a risk that Yuri had blocked his dad's access to Mission Control. Thankfully, he hadn't, because the door to the delivery area opened immediately.

"I guess Yuri thought we were toast," said Jack's dad with a grin.

As they entered the room, Jack and his dad quickly crouched down low. His father was right about it being a delivery area, but wrong about the fact that nobody would be at work.

Jack counted at least five men, two

driving forklifts and three on the floor. Across the room, he spied a door with a sign above it saying, THIS WAY TO MISSION CONTROL ROOM.

Jack nodded to his dad that he would go first. He hunched over and ran to a nearby stack of boxes, then waited a few seconds before calling his dad over. When he made it, Jack sighed in relief. And so it went on, until the two Stalwarts reached the opposite door.

Jack's dad placed his thumb on another black thumbprint box. The door opened, and the pair dashed from the delivery area into a long hallway.

"Where to next?" asked Jack. His dad knew the place better than almost anyone.

"This way," said his dad, pointing down the hallway toward another door.

When they got to it, they pushed it open and stepped through.

Chapter 13:
The Surprise

Thankfully, there was so much going on in the room that when the Stalwarts entered, nobody seemed to notice. They scurried around the back and found a corner hidden from sight.

Jack glanced at his Watch Phone. It was ten minutes until the launch. He took out his Google Goggles, set them to "maximum length" and furtively glanced around for Yuri.

Jack's dad looked at him. "Are those from Hong Kong too?" he asked.

"No," whispered Jack. "I got them from a shop selling toy spy gadgets. But they work really well."

As Jack scanned the room, he noticed a large glass viewing box on the first floor. Yuri was standing inside watching over Mission Control. A man came in and greeted Yuri. Jack grabbed his Ear Amp from his Book Bag and quickly plunged it

into his ear. He tapped on it twice to increase its hearing distance. Listening carefully, Jack tried to make out what they were saying.

"We're almost there," said Yuri. "Without you, we wouldn't have the code."

"No problem, boss," said the other man. "It's been my pleasure to serve you."

Jack guessed the other man was Alexei, the hacker.

As Jack watched Yuri, he saw him walk to a microphone mounted on a desk. Yuri flipped a switch, and then began to speak.

"Team!" he said. "In ten minutes, we will make history! Everybody take your positions."

The Ear Amp was so sensitive to noise that the sound of Yuri's voice roared into Jack's ears. Shaking and smacking his head sideways, Jack forced the Ear Amp to fall out.

Jack and his dad watched as the workers did as they were told. They walked to their stations and prepared for liftoff.

"I need to get to the control panel," said Jack's dad. "There might be a way to lock the keypad and stop Yuri from entering the code."

"Okay," said Jack. "I'll keep a close eye on Yuri." But before he let his dad go, he tried to give him some advice. "Try to keep low," he whispered to him. "We don't want anyone to know we're here."

Jack's father nodded in agreement, and then scurried to a desk across from the control panel. He crouched down just beside it, and when the woman who was working at it walked away, he made his way over to the panel itself.

When Jack saw his dad touching some buttons, he figured he was disabling the keypad as planned. Jack was finally starting to relax.

But just when things were going their way, Jack heard a loud scream from the front of the room. It was Vigo, and he was carrying what looked like a Super Soaker.

Before Jack could do anything, Vigo lifted it up and pointed it in the direction of his dad. He'd been spotted! A powerful light burst out of the front and into Jack's dad, throwing him backward. His father crashed through some computer monitors and fell hard onto the carpeted floor.

Vigo ran toward Jack's father as everyone in the control room screamed and ducked for cover. The Russian roughly grabbed John Stalwart and began to cart him away. Jack looked at Yuri, who was watching everything from above. Leaning close to the microphone again, Yuri made another announcement.

"Don't worry, ladies and gentlemen," he said. "As I told you, John Stalwart has gone a bit mad. We are taking him back to the hospital now. The light that you saw," he added, "has merely stunned him. He'll be all right in a few minutes."

People looked around at one another nervously. "Please, everybody," said Yuri, "get back to work. Don't forget, we have to make John proud and launch his rocket."

Jack was really fuming now. Yuri was using his dad's name to cheer these people on into launching the rocket! Jack knew his dad was only stunned, but it didn't matter. Anyone who hurt a member of the Stalwart family was going to regret it. Jack would make sure of that.

Chapter 14:
The Only One

Jack watched Vigo as he carried his dad to the glass box upstairs and strapped him to a chair for the second time. They clearly had no intention of taking him to a hospital. Jack guessed Yuri wanted to keep a closer eye on his father, but at least he wasn't looking for Jack.

Glancing at his Watch Phone, Jack felt a slight twinge of panic. There were only five minutes left until Yuri would try to enter the code.

Jack thought through his options. He could call the Russian police, but Mars Mission Control was miles from anywhere. If he called them, they would probably be too late.

He could summon the security guards on site, but Jack wasn't sure whether they could be trusted. After all, Yuri was a powerful man, and Jack didn't know how many others Yuri had working for him on his sinister plans.

Another option was to rescue his dad and get him to try and block the keypad again. But that would take time—time that Jack didn't have.

The only person Jack could count on was himself. And the only way to stop the launch was to let Yuri enter the code. Only when the countdown started could Jack press the EMERGENCY SHUTDOWN button. As his dad said, it was the final way to completely stop the rocket launch. But he still needed to get to the control panel without being seen. Jack sat back in the corner and started thinking of a new plan.

Chapter 15:
The Cat's Attack

For some reason, Jack started to think about his GPF instructor Mr. Dee's survival class. In it, he taught recruits to think and act like animals when it came to attack. Jack liked to pretend to be a cat. He could lie in wait, and then pounce on someone when he was least expected.

This thought gave him an idea about how to stop Yuri and the Mars mission launch. He looked around. Next to him was a steel column that rose to a beam near the ceiling.

"Perfect," he said to himself.

Opening the sole on his left shoe, Jack took out two blue pellets. These were the GPF's Smoke- Screen Pellets. He then took two sheets of Sticky Treads and placed the sheets on the bottom of his shoes.

With his hands free, he reached into his Book Bag for his KlimbKit and clipped it to his belt. Then he grabbed his Gripper Gloves and slipped one onto each hand.

Jack placed his hands around the steel column nearby and, using the Sticky Treads and the grip of his gloves, he climbed to the top. By the time he got

there, his arms and legs were aching, but from that position he could see the whole of Mars Mission Control. It was perfect for his plan.

It was 7:26 A.M., and Yuri and Alexei were leaving the glass box and walking downstairs. Jack looked over to his dad, who was finally coming around. He tried to signal to him, but unfortunately, his dad didn't see him.

As Yuri and Alexei reached the control panel, the clock flicked over to 7:27 A.M. It was only three minutes until liftoff.

Looking around the room, Jack couldn't find Vigo anywhere. After he'd tied up John Stalwart, he'd left the glass box and was nowhere to be seen.

Jack watched the time tick down. When it reached thirty seconds to countdown, he opened his KlimbKit. Positioning it where he wanted it to go, Jack pushed the EJECT button. A thin but strong string shot out from inside and wrapped itself around one of the rafters. He tugged on it, making sure it was secure.

After Yuri punched in the code, a woman's voice came over the loud speaker: *"Mission launch has been activated."*

The crowd of workers clapped and cheered.

Now was Jack's only chance. He had to activate the emergency button before the countdown reached zero. Leaping from the beam, Jack swung through Mission Control like Spiderman.

Aiming for the control desk, he let himself fall, landing on Yuri and Alexei and knocking them down.

"Owww!" yelled Yuri as he crumpled under Jack's weight.

"Urggh!" groaned Alexei, who'd been thrown on his side.

"Rocket to lift off in ten . . . nine . . ."

There was no time to waste. Jack stepped over Yuri's face and made his way toward the control desk. He spied the EMERGENCY SHUTDOWN button and put his hand out. But just as he was about to push it, something came flying at him from the side.

Alexei ploughed into Jack, throwing him onto the floor.

"Eight . . . seven . . ."

Jack could hear the rocket boosters roar over the loud speaker. The Mars spacecraft was about to take off.

Yuri and Alexei gathered together in front of the desk. They were blocking Jack from going anywhere near the emergency button.

"Go ahead and try that again!" shouted Yuri.

"Six . . . five . . ."

"Come on!" yelled Yuri, wanting Jack to strike.

"Two against one sounds pretty fair!" squealed Alexei.

"Four . . . three . . ."

Jack was breathing heavily now. There were only two seconds left. He reached into his trouser pocket and pulled out his Smoke-Screen Pellets, then threw one at Yuri's cheek and the other toward Alexei's nose. As soon as they hit, the pellets stuck and burst open, releasing a dark blue smoke in front of their eyes. Yuri and Alexei couldn't see a thing.

The Russians frantically shook their heads, trying to get the pellets off. But GPF Smoke-Screen Pellets don't come off easily, at least not until after two minutes.

Jack ran around the blinded men and clambered onto the desk. The men's hands were swooping wildly in an attempt to catch him.

"*Two . . .*"

Within that second, Jack saw the button again. He pushed it as quickly as he could.

Just then, a horrible noise blared through Mission Control. Jack wondered if the rocket was blasting off.

BEEP!

BEEP!

BEEP!

The computerized voice came over the speaker again.

"*Emergency shutdown has been activated. Liftoff has been canceled.*"

It took a few seconds to register, but Jack had done it. He'd stopped the rocket from taking off!

"Noooo!" yelled a familiar voice. It was Vigo. The third Russian had come back.

FLASH!

A burst of light went off.

FLASH!

And then another.

Vigo was zapping anything in sight with the light gun. Jack crouched down out of the way. People were fleeing everywhere. He saw Vigo running toward Yuri and Alexei, who were still struggling to see through the thick blue smoke.

As the three Russians stood together, Jack smiled. He pulled his Net Tosser out of his Book Bag and threw it in the direction of the men, where it broke open and cast a net over the thugs.

Vigo pulled the trigger on his gun, but the burst of light bounced back at them from the Net Tosser's bulletproof walls.

"Owww!" screeched Yuri as the heat of the light burned off one of his eyebrows.

At that moment, the doors at the back of Mission Control were flung open and a team of Russian police stormed through. Jack was confused. He hadn't called anyone yet.

"You're not the only one with clever ideas," said a voice from behind him. Jack turned around. It was his dad.

"Dad!" said Jack, completely stunned. The last time he'd seen his dad, he was tied to a chair. "But how did you escape?" he asked.

"I was able to free myself by hopping over to some scissors on Yuri's desk," Jack's dad replied.

Jack was totally impressed. It must have been his dad who'd called the cops. In the end, they hadn't taken that long to arrive. Jack threw his arms around his father and gave him a hug.

"I'm proud of you, son," John Stalwart said. "Without you, the rocket would have gone into space,

and those astronauts might have died."
He let out a big sigh. "We'll have to phone
your mum—she must be worried sick. I'll
make a call and book you on the next
flight out of Moscow. It's time we got you
home."

Chapter 16:
The Mind Game

While they were talking, Jack made a few taps on his wrist. The Net Tosser released its grip, and the cops swarmed over to the men. They cuffed Yuri, Alexei and Vigo and hauled them away.

All in all, Jack thought, things couldn't have turned out better. But it was about that time in every mission when Jack had to find a secret way home.

"Dad," he said, "can I see you over

here?" He led his dad over to a quiet corner of the room.

"I thought you'd appreciate this," he said, giving him a box that he'd pulled from his Book Bag. "It's another one of Richard's latest toys."

"Okay," said his dad, taking the box in his hand.

"Now, look into the middle," said Jack, "and tell me what you see."

"All I can see is something swirling inside," he replied.

"Perfect," said Jack. "Keep looking at it. This really is an amazing gadget. I promise."

Jack's dad was slowly being transfixed by the GPF's Mind Eraser. It was the most powerful tool for erasing somebody's short-term memory. Although he hated doing it, Jack couldn't let his dad remember he was there. The only other people who knew about Jack were the three Russians, and no one would believe those criminals.

With his dad distracted, Jack slipped out unnoticed through the back door. Outside, he could see Yuri, Alexei and Vigo being thrown into the back of a Russian police van. When the doors to the van slammed shut, Jack moved around the building to a quiet space.

He pulled out his foldaway map and opened it onto the ground. Then he touched the outline of England and waited for the light inside to fire up.

When it did, he yelled, "Off to England!" The map swallowed him whole and sent him back to the New Forest.

Chapter 17:
The Return to Earth

When Jack arrived, he found himself in the exact spot from where he'd left. He tucked his portable Magic Map into his Book Bag, and tapped his Watch Phone for the latest GPF news. He hit the video button so he could see a live report.

Evelyn Lewis, chief reporter for the GPF, was there in Moscow's Red Square.

"Yuri Ivanov, the commander of the Mars Mission Team, was arrested in

Russia today on a number of charges, including kidnapping, command of a deadly light weapon and knowingly trying to send astronauts into space in an unsafe spacecraft. Vigo Popov and Alexei Smirnov were also arrested. Secret Agent 'Courage' assisted in the capture and arrest of all three men.

"As a consequence of Mr. Ivanov's criminal behavior, John Stalwart was named the new commander of the Mars Mission Team.

" 'I'm proud to serve this team as their new commander," said Mr. Stalwart. 'Once we've added the appropriate safeguards to the craft,' he added, 'we plan to send the first man to Mars.'

"When asked who assisted in the capture of Yuri Ivanov, Mr. Stalwart shook his head and admitted, 'It's strange, but I really can't remember what happened.' "

Jack logged out of his Watch Phone and headed back to where Richard and Charlie were lying. He sat down beside his friends and took a few moments to think about the mission.

Not only had he nabbed three bad guys, he'd saved the astronauts and helped his dad land his dream job. And he'd done it all without his father remembering a thing. For now, Jack's secret was safe from his family.

"So, did you survive?" asked Richard.

Jack froze. How did he know? Did someone see something?

"You know, your trip to the restroom?" Richard continued.

Jack breathed a sigh of relief. "Barely," he said, trying to be funny. "Almost flushed myself down the toilet."

At that the three friends started to howl with laughter. It was funny, Jack thought—friends always had a habit of bringing each other down to earth.

The Quest for
Aztec Gold:
MEXICO

BOOK (10)

The Quest for Aztec Gold: MEXICO

Elizabeth Singer Hunt

Illustrated by Brian Williamson

WEINSTEIN BOOKS

ISBN: 978-1-60286-079-7

First Edition
10   9   8   7   6

For Elizabeth and Felicity

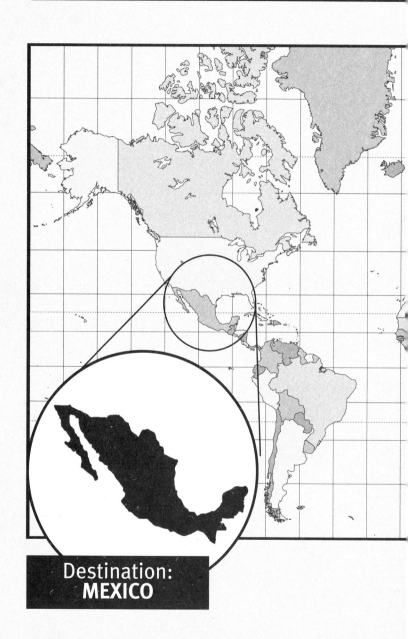

Destination:
MEXICO

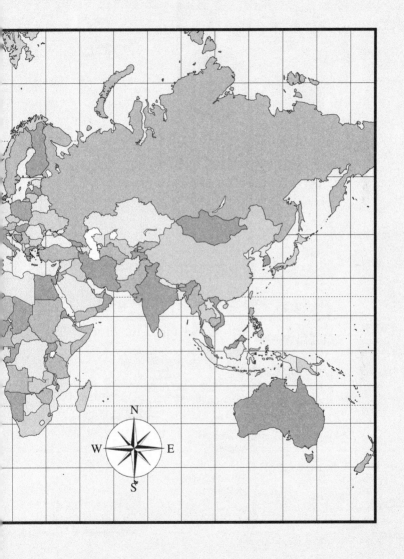

Jack Stalwart applied to be a secret agent for the Global Protection Force four months ago.

My name is Jack Stalwart. My older brother, Max, was a secret agent for you, until he disappeared on one of your missions. Now I want to be a secret agent too. If you choose me, I will be an excellent secret agent and get rid of evil villains, just like my brother did. Sincerely,

Jack Stalwart

HIGHLY CONFIDENTIAL

Jack Stalwart was sworn in as a Global Protection Force secret agent four months ago. Since that time, he has completed all of his missions successfully and has stopped no less than twelve evil villains. Because of this he has been assigned the code name "COURAGE."

Jack has yet to uncover the whereabouts of his brother, Max, who is still working for this organization at a secret location. Do not give Secret Agent Jack Stalwart this information. He is never to know about his brother.

Gerald Barter

Gerald Barter
Director, Global Protection Force

THINGS YOU'LL FIND IN EVERY BOOK

Watch Phone: The only gadget Jack wears all the time, even when he's not on official business. His Watch Phone is the central gadget that makes most others work. There are lots of important features, most importantly the "C" button, which reveals the code of the day—necessary to unlock Jack's Secret Agent Book Bag. There are buttons on both sides, one of which ejects his life-saving Melting Ink Pen. Beyond these functions, it also works as a phone and, of course, gives Jack the time of day.

Global Protection Force (GPF): The GPF is the organization Jack works for. It's a worldwide force of young secret agents whose aim is to protect the world's people, places and possessions. No one knows exactly where its main offices are located (all correspondence and gadgets for repair are sent to a special PO Box, and training is held at various locations around the world), but Jack thinks it's somewhere cold, like the Arctic Circle.

Whizzy: Jack's magical miniature globe. Almost every night at precisely 7:30 P.M., the GPF uses Whizzy to send Jack the identity of the country that he must travel to. Whizzy can't talk, but he can cough up messages. Jack's parents don't know Whizzy is anything more than a normal globe.

The Magic Map: The magical map hanging on Jack's bedroom wall. Unlike most maps, the GPF's map is made of a mysterious wood. Once Jack inserts the country piece from Whizzy, the map swallows Jack whole and sends him away on his missions. When he returns, he arrives precisely one minute after he left.

Secret Agent Book Bag: The Book Bag that Jack wears on every adventure. Licensed only to GPF secret agents, it contains top-secret gadgets necessary to foil bad guys and escape certain death. To activate the bag before each mission, Jack must punch in a secret code given to him by his Watch Phone. Once he's away, all he has to do is place his finger on the zipper, which identifies him as the owner of the bag and immediately opens.

THE STALWART FAMILY

Jack's dad, John

He moved the family to England when Jack was two, in order to take a job with an aerospace company. Jack's dad thinks he is an ordinary boy and that his other son, Max, attends a school in Switzerland. Jack's dad is American and his mum is British, which makes Jack a bit of both.

Jack's mum, Corinne

One of the greatest mums as far as Jack is concerned. When she and her husband received a letter from a posh school in Switzerland inviting Max to attend, they were overjoyed. Since Max left six months ago, they have received numerous notes in Max's handwriting telling them he's OK. Little do they know it's all a lie and that it's the GPF sending those letters.

Jack's older brother, Max

Two years ago, at the age of nine, Max joined the GPF. Max used to tell Jack about his adventures and show him how to work his secret-agent gadgets. When the family received a letter inviting Max to attend a school in Europe, Jack figured it was to do with the GPF. Max told him he was right, but that he couldn't tell Jack anything about why he was going away.

Nine-year-old Jack Stalwart

Four months ago, Jack received an anonymous note saying: "Your brother is in danger. Only you can save him." As soon as he could, Jack applied to be a secret agent too. Since that time, he's battled some of the world's most dangerous villains, and hopes some day in his travels to find and rescue his brother, Max.

DESTINATION:
Mexico

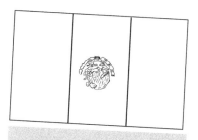

Mexico is the world's largest Spanish-speaking country.

◻

It is on the continent of North America.

◻

More than 100 million people live there.

The north of Mexico has deserts, the south has many jungles.

◻

The capital city of Mexico is Mexico City.

◻

Mexico's currency is the Peso.

THE AZTEC CIVILIZATION: FACTS AND FIGURES

The word "Aztec" is used to describe an ancient people who shared customs and spoke the Nahuatl language.

The Aztecs ate mainly corn, beans, chillis and tomatoes. They also ate grasshoppers and ants!

Their capital city was called Tenochtitlán (pronounced Te-noch-tit-lan), which was destroyed by the Spanish in 1521.

In 1978, Tenochtitlán was rediscovered by some electricity workers who stumbled upon a stone carving and started excavating.

GPF Fact File:
Hernán Cortés and the Spanish

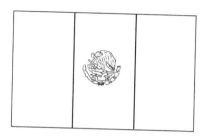

Hernán Cortés was part of a
group of Spanish "conquistadores"
who took control of lands
on behalf of their
Emperor Charles V.

In 1519, Cortes landed on present-day
Mexico and began to march
with his men toward
Tenochtitlán.

After tricking the ruler of the Aztecs,
Montezuma II, Cortés imprisoned
and killed him.

After that, the Spanish took over.
All but 5 percent of the original Aztecs
died from fighting and smallpox,
a disease the Spanish brought
to Mexico.

Cortés ruled Mexico until 1524.

Mexico received its independence
from Spain three centuries later,
in 1821.

AZTEC SYMBOLS

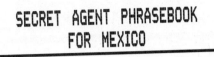

SECRET AGENT PHRASEBOOK
FOR MEXICO

What is your name?
¿Cómo te llamas?
(pronounced Ko-mo tay ya-mas)

My name is
Me llamo
(pronounced May-yamo)

Goodbye
Adios
(pronounced A-dee-os)

Hello
Hola
(pronounced O-la)

How are you?
¿Cómo estás?
(pronounced Ko-mo a-stas)

OK
Bien
(pronounced Bee-en)

SECRET AGENT GADGET INSTRUCTION MANUAL

 **Double A Device:** If you're looking for information on or the location of an ancient site, use the GPF's Double A Device. Just type in what you know (key words or phrases) and this handheld gadget will try to help you out. Great for getting clues on the whereabouts of a lost city or for mapping current archaeological digs.

 **Abseil Kit:** When there's no other way down a mountain or rock face, use the GPF's Abseil Kit. The kit includes ropes, a harness and an abseil anchor. You will also need your Noggin Mold. Attempt to descend only if you've attended Mr. Kennedy's abseil training class.

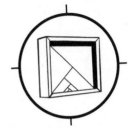

Portable Map: Small enough to fit in your Book Bag, this wooden square opens up to the size of your Magic Map. Just place the jigsaw piece inside as normal and it will transport you home or to your next mission.

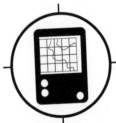

Map Mate: When you're lost or need to get somewhere fast, use the GPF's Map Mate. This clever gadget receives signals from satellites in space to give you a map of any country, city or town in the world. It can also show you how to get from one place to another using directional arrows to guide the way.

Chapter 1:
The Chase

Secret Agent Jack Stalwart was running for his life. He was sprinting across an open plain, trying to escape from four dark shadows that were chasing him at top speed.

Jack spied a prickly bush up ahead. Rather than run around it, he jumped right over.

BLAM!

His feet crashed to the ground, spraying sandy dust into the air.

1

BLAM! BLAM! BLAM! BLAM!

The shadows jumped too, grunting as they landed. It felt as though they were close enough to almost touch Jack. But he was still a few seconds ahead.

Reaching for his Book Bag, he tried to grab one of his life-saving gadgets. But Jack's Book Bag wasn't on his back. Strange, he thought. It was always there.

Out of nowhere, Jack stumbled. He fell forward, his hands slamming into the sand. He rolled over several times and tried to get himself upright. But the shadows soon reached him, howling with evil laughter.

"Noooo!" Jack screamed, as the dark figures leaned over and . . .

Chapter 2:
The Hunter

"Noooo!" Jack yelled again, and sat bolt upright in his bed at home. He was sweating and shaking. Confused, Jack looked around.

It was definitely his bedroom. Whizzy was asleep on his bedside table. The clock next to Whizzy said 7:15 P.M., and Jack's Magic Map was still on his wall. What had seemed like a real life-or-death chase was nothing more than a bad dream.

Feeling something leaning against his stomach, he reached down to pick it up. It was a book called *The Most Dangerous Treasure Hunters in the World*. That would explain the nightmare, he thought. Jack had dozed off before his normal bedtime while reading about the adventures of the notorious treasure hunter, Callous Carl.

Callous Carl ruled the southern part of America when it came to treasure hunting. If there was gold to find, Callous Carl and his gang of bandits weren't too far behind.

He had been given the name "Callous" because he was heartless and because years of digging up gold had turned his hands rough, like sandpaper. Although nobody knew exactly how many men worked for Carl, there were estimates he had up to ten men in his gang.

The book had a description of the chief outlaw.

Carl was missing a right eyebrow, and he wore beat-up cowboy clothes and red leather boots. He carried a pointed dagger in a sheath on his hip. Callous Carl definitely belonged in Jack's book. He was one dangerous dude.

"Are you okay?" said a voice, as a knock came from the other side of Jack's door. It was Jack's mother. She must have heard him shout out. She opened the door a crack, and stuck her face around it.

"I'm okay, Mum," said Jack, holding up his book. "I fell asleep while reading this, and I guess it gave me a nightmare."

"Glad you're all right," she said. "Just make sure to get yourself ready for bed. It's almost seven thirty. Love you," she added, as she blew him a kiss and closed the door.

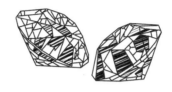

Chapter 3:
The Setting

With the fright of the dream, Jack had forgotten the time. It was almost 7:30 P.M., and he was about to find out whether he was off on a mission tonight.

Although his parents and friends thought he was an ordinary boy, Jack was actually a secret agent. He worked for the Global Protection Force, or GPF, an organization whose role was to protect the world's most precious treasures.

Whether it was stopping a thug from stealing the Rosetta Stone, or an animal trafficker from selling endangered species, nothing was too difficult for a GPF agent.

In the four short months since Jack was sworn in, he'd stopped no less than twelve evil criminals. That's why the GPF gave him the code name "Courage," which, not coincidentally, was also the meaning of his surname, "Stalwart."

As the clock changed over to 7:30 P.M., Whizzy, Jack's GPF globe, began to twirl. As Whizzy spun around and around, Jack watched him reach top speed. Whizzy coughed—Ahem!—and a jigsaw piece flew out of his mouth.

This one was large, thought Jack, as he recognized its shape. Rushing over, Jack picked it up and carried it to the Magic Map on his wall. Placing it to the south of the USA, Jack slipped the piece in and stepped back. The name MEXICO appeared in the middle of the country and then disappeared.

He wondered what was going wrong in that country. Perhaps there was something amiss at the Zócalo, the main square in Mexico City. Or maybe there was danger on the beaches of Cancún.

Knowing there wasn't much time, Jack hurried over to his bed. He knelt down and lifted up his bedsheets. Spying his GPF Book Bag underneath, he pulled it out, and asked his Watch Phone for the code of the day.

When it played back FIESTA, he keyed it into the lock on his Book Bag, and instantly, the lock popped open. Rummaging through, he noticed the Flyboard was there, as was the Map Mate. There were also some new gadgets in there, like the Double-A Device and the Abseil Kit. Jack had read about them in the *GPF Electronic News* and was anxious to see whether he could use them on his upcoming mission.

Putting everything away, he tossed his Book Bag over his shoulders and ran back in front of the Magic Map. As the white light grew from inside the country, he waited until the time was right. When it was, he yelled "Off to Mexico!" The brilliant light exploded and swallowed Jack into the Magic Map.

Chapter 4:
The Assignment

When Jack arrived in Mexico, he found himself in the middle of a dry and dusty terrain. There was hard earth under his feet, and scrubby bushes dotted the plains. Since he knew that a lot of southern Mexico was covered in rain forest, he figured he was somewhere between the middle and the north of the country.

Up ahead, he could see a collection of

one-story wooden houses. Thinking that
whoever had called the GPF was in one of
them, he made his way for the closest
one. As he approached the house, he
looked through the window and noticed
there was someone inside. From what
Jack could tell it was an elderly Mexican
man. The man was sitting in a rocking
chair in his den. When he spied Jack, he
waved furiously for him to come in.

Thinking this was his contact, Jack
walked to the front door. Rather than just
open it, he knocked, to be polite.

"*Habla inglés?*" Jack called out,
checking whether the man spoke English.

"Yes," said the voice inside. "Come
in . . . come in!"

Jack turned the handle and pushed the
door open. He found himself standing in
a cozy, tidy house.

15

"Come in," the man said again, telling Jack to join him in the den. Jack made himself comfortable in a squishy brown leather chair.

The old man was tall and thin, and had wavy white hair and a thick bushy mustache. Jack guessed his age was about seventy.

"The name is José Garcia," he said, holding out his right hand toward Jack.

Jack put out his hand too and introduced himself. When the two had finished their greeting, the man got up as if he were headed off somewhere. "*Café*

con leche?" he asked. He wanted to make Jack something to drink.

"No thanks," said Jack. He didn't want to be rude, but while some kids at home were allowed to drink coffee with milk, he didn't like it much.

"So," said the man, sitting back down. "Shall I tell you why I called the GPF?"

"Yes," said Jack, anxious to hear about his mission. He wondered what on earth this old man could need from the GPF organization.

"Someone has stolen something from me," the man said. "Something more than five hundred years old." This grabbed Jack's attention. Anything that old was classified as an antique. Whatever it was, it was worthy of full GPF protection.

"What is it?" asked Jack.

"A map," replied Mr. Garcia. "The lost map of Montezuma's gold."

Chapter 5:
The First Clue

Jack nearly fell off his chair. If what the man was saying was true, then this was a very special mission indeed. Montezuma II was the ancient ruler of the Aztec people, who lived on the land between Mexico and Honduras from the fourteenth to the sixteenth century.

In 1519, the Spanish landed on the coast of Mexico and marched to the Aztec city of Tenochtitlán. They conquered it, making sure that Montezuma was killed in the process.

There were rumors that before the Spanish arrived, Montezuma had his men hide much of his wealth. While the Spanish made off with whatever they could find in the city, the whereabouts of this gold had tempted treasure hunters for years.

"Where did you get the map?" asked Jack. He was a bit suspicious. A map as legendary as this would not normally be sitting in some old guy's house in the middle of Mexico.

"My good friend, Carlos Ortega, is a renowned archaeologist. Ever heard of him?" Mr. Garcia asked, raising his eyebrows at Jack.

Unfortunately, he hadn't. Jack shook his head.

"Well," the man explained, "he was one

of the principal archaeologists at the dig at Tenochtitlán."

Jack had heard something about this in Mrs. Butterworth's GPF archaeology tutorial. In the 1970s, an electricity worker discovered a precious Aztec stone. Scientists did some digging around that stone and unearthed the ancient Aztec city of Tenochtitlán, buried under present-day Mexico City.

Since then, archaeologists had been excavating it bit by bit. Recently, they'd found the Templo Mayor, where Aztec priests performed human sacrifices.

"Ortega found the treasure map on a scroll hidden in one of the walls of the palace," Mr. Garcia explained, "and gave it to me to watch."

"Why you?" asked Jack.

"Because I'm a trustworthy guy," he replied, grinning. "And he wanted it as far away from Mexico City as possible."

"Why?" asked Jack, who didn't understand why Mr. Ortega didn't just put it away in a bank vault or inside a museum.

"Because he didn't want to be associated with it," he said. "He knew greedy people would hound him for it. And if he showed it to any of his fellow archaeologists, they would want to put it in a museum."

"What's wrong with that?" asked Jack. Museums, as far as he was concerned, were the best places for things like this.

"Well, because then the map would be on show!" he said. "It would be like a calling card to all treasure hunters: 'Come and see the map of Montezuma's gold!'"

Jack wasn't sure he agreed with Carlos Ortega's reasoning, but the fact was that someone had gotten their hands on the map. Jack figured he needed more information to find out who it could be.

"Is there anybody living in the house besides you?" asked Jack.

"No, just me," said Mr. Garcia. "My wife passed away many years ago."

"Does somebody help you clean your house?" asked Jack.

"Maria comes every other week," he said.

Jack thought this was interesting. Maybe this Maria had something to do with the theft. "Where does she live?" Jack asked.

"Two towns over," said the man. "But Maria is a very nice girl," he explained. "She would have had nothing to do with it."

"So where did you keep the map?" asked Jack. Although Mr. Garcia thought Maria was in the clear, Jack was keeping her in mind as a possible suspect.

"In a cookie jar in the kitchen," said the man.

Jack couldn't help but grimace. He couldn't believe something that precious had been kept in a cookie jar!

Seeing Jack's reaction, the man chimed in, "Seemed like the safest place to me! After all," he added, "who would keep something that important in a cookie jar?"

Exactly, thought Jack, but said aloud: "When did you notice it was missing?"

"This morning," Mr. Garcia replied, "when I got up to make my *café con leche*. I check the jar every day," he added, "and today the jar itself was gone."

"You did the right thing, calling the GPF," said Jack. "Mind if I take a look?" Jack wanted to see if there were any clues in the kitchen.

"By all means," said the old man.

Jack left Mr. Garcia and walked into the other room. As the man said, there was no cookie jar anywhere to be found. But there weren't any signs of forced entry—no broken windows or upturned furniture.

Returning to the den, Jack started to wonder if this old man was mad. Perhaps he had made the whole thing up.

"Do you remember what the map looks like?" asked Jack.

"I do," said the man. "I made a careful note of it in my brain."

Not sure whether the man's brain was all there, Jack figured he had no other choice but to try to pick it.

"Can you draw a picture of what you remember?" asked Jack.

The man grabbed a piece of paper and pen from his desk. As he started to doodle, he added, "You know, it was made from the flattened bark of a fig tree. It was very fragile."

Jack knew that the ancient Aztecs did use the bark of fig trees as paper. The fact that this man knew that told Jack that maybe he wasn't loony after all.

"Here you go," said the man, handing the piece of paper over to Jack.

As Jack looked down at the drawing, he

was amazed at what he saw. There before him was a drawing of a possible treasure map.

At the bottom was a picture of a horse with a long tail. Just above that was a picture of a building on top of a hill. Lastly, there was a picture of a triangular structure with a crescent moon on top.

Jack knew that the Aztecs used drawings instead of words to tell stories and count. Perhaps, thought Jack, they decided to use pictures to give the location of the buried treasure.

Jack knew something else about Aztec drawings. They placed things on top of one another to show distance. This meant the picture on the bottom was a possible starting point, with every picture on top farther away geographically.

But why were there several pictures, instead of just one? It would have been easier to give one clue to the location of the buried treasure. Maybe, Jack reasoned, there was a purpose in all of this. Perhaps there was something to see or collect at each place.

Jack figured one other thing too. Whoever had their hands on the map now was thinking the same. And given that they might have taken the map this morning, that meant they were at least a few hours ahead of Jack in locating the treasure.

Jack looked again at the first drawing. He thought it was curious that Mr. Garcia had drawn the horse's tail so long. "Was the horse's tail really this long?" asked Jack.

The old man nodded his head.

"Was there anything else unusual?" asked Jack. "Were the hairs on the tail thick, or perhaps painted a particular color?"

"Now that you mention it," said the man, "the horse's tail was blue. I thought that was pretty odd at the time, since most horsehairs are black or brown."

"Exactly," said Jack, who had an idea. Blue was the universally recognized color for water.

"Are there any waterfalls in Mexico where the water flows out like this?" asked Jack, pointing to the direction indicated by the tail.

"There's a waterfall east of here, in Monterrey," he offered. "Now you mention it, the water does flow in a similar arc."

"Perfect," said Jack, who was feeling confident at this new lead. "I'll find the map, and when I do, I'll make sure it comes back to you."

"Good luck on your journey," said Mr. Garcia.

"*Adios*," said Jack as he hurried out the door.

Chapter 6:
The Route

As soon as he left the old man's house, Jack pulled his Map Mate out of his bag. The GPF's Map Mate was a hand-held navigation device that gave you directions from one place to another, anywhere in the world.

What made the Map Mate so special was that it didn't need to have roads to guide you. It could give you directions over any type of terrain including jungles, deserts or even ice. The Map Mate always knew where you were and where you were going. All the agent had to do was follow the arrows.

After Jack programmed in the name "Monterrey," the Map Mate calculated Jack's route. According to the device, Jack needed to go eighty kilometers, or almost fifty miles, east. Looking around him, Jack couldn't see any public transport options and there was no way he could walk that far: he needed to get there fast!

Plucking his Flyboard out of his Book Bag, he placed the gadget on the ground. The GPF's Flyboard looked like a skateboard, only it used hydrogen-powered jets instead of feet to make it go. The Flyboard could carry an agent at a speed of twenty-five miles per hour as it hovered a yard off the ground.

Jack turned on the Flyboard by tapping

a few commands on his Watch Phone. Once he'd strapped his Anti-detection Visor over his eyes and Noggin Mold to his head, he stepped on. Within moments, Jack was moving east toward Monterrey and possibly the first clue on the map.

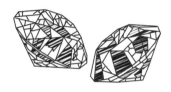

Chapter 7:
The Forest

As Jack and the Flyboard entered the
area, he noticed that this part of Mexico
was greener than the land around Mr.
Garcia's house. It was also rugged, with
steep cliffs, mountains and canyons.

The arrow on the Map Mate was
flashing, telling Jack he was getting close.
It looked like he needed to find a route
through the small forest ahead.

When he reached the trees, he hopped

off the Flyboard and put away his protective gear. Ducking under some overgrown foliage, he stepped onto a muddy path. There, behind some leafy bushes was an old, wooden sign.

Although most of the sign's paint had been washed away, Jack could still make out a few words. It said, COLA DE CABALLO. Jack knew that meant "horse's tail" in Spanish. This was the path Jack was looking for.

He climbed the trail for about thirty yards, until he came to a clearing. There, in the middle of an open space, was a large pool of water. The pond was surrounded by a circle of rocks. The circle wasn't man-made; the rocks had been left by nature.

When the water in the pool got too high, it flowed over the rocks and down a steep hill. In doing so, it made a small waterfall that dropped below to another pool. But this wasn't the waterfall Jack was here to view. It was the one crashing from above, and it was absolutely beautiful.

As Jack craned his neck to see, the spray from the waterfall above sprinkled on his face. The water started from a narrow opening at the top of a cliff. As it poured out over the rocks in its way, it fanned out so that it looked just like the horse's tail in the drawing.

Sure that the picture of the horse must represent the waterfall, Jack thought about what to do next. He wondered whether the Aztecs had buried something important nearby. Or, whether the waterfall was the first part of a larger clue. Thinking that anything was possible, Jack started looking around.

He searched the side of the water that he was on, but he couldn't find a thing. There was nothing carved into any of the rocks, and nothing on any of the trees or bushes.

Knowing he had to get to the other side, Jack thought about his choices. He could walk over the rocks at the bottom edge, but one slip could send him tumbling down the next waterfall.

Or, he could swim across the pool itself. His clothes would eventually dry off, and his Book Bag and boots were waterproof. Jack climbed over one of the rocks and lowered himself into the chilly water. He was used to swimming in cool temperatures. What he wasn't used to was the feeling of something slimy swimming up his trousers.

Hoping it was a friendly fish rather than anything more dangerous, Jack continued to swim to the other side. Clambering over the rocks and onto dry land, Jack squeezed a bit of water out of his trousers and began to look around.

As he did, he saw something interesting. Behind the waterfall itself, he spied what looked like a cave. It had been hidden from view before, but now Jack could see it clearly. Shaking some water out of his ears, Jack made his way over to it.

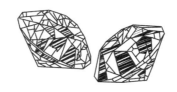

Chapter 8:
The Cave

As Jack approached the cave's entrance, he thought he could hear noises. Pulling away quickly, he stood with his back tight against the outside wall. Carefully, he craned his neck around the corner to see what was going on.

Inside the cave were five men. Four of them were stashing pickaxes and other tools into a burlap bag, while another man was giving orders.

"Hurry up!" shouted the leader. "We've got to get a move on if we're gonna find that gold!"

The others grunted and cackled with laughter. From what Jack could see, one or two of the men were missing their front teeth.

So, thought Jack, these were the guys. These were the men who had stolen the map from Mr. Garcia's house. Only thing was, he still couldn't figure out how they'd done it. Jack wondered whether they had already found something in the cave—something linked to Montezuma's treasure.

"Gather up that water too!" the leader yelled, still barking commands. "We've got a long day ahead. We're heading south." One of the men scurried to a corner of the cave and grabbed a few bottles.

So the mysterious men were heading

south, but where? Jack hadn't had a chance to properly study the next clue on the map.

Jack followed the bossy man with his eyes. Until now, he'd had his back turned to Jack, so he hadn't seen his face.

The man walked to the back of the cave. There on the far wall was what looked like a freshly made hole. The man

grabbed a knife from his hip pocket.
Using the tip, he picked a small red stone
out of the wall. It looked like a ruby. As it
came out of the wall, the stone fell into
his hand.

Placing the jewel in a small bag clipped
to his trousers, the man turned around
and returned to his men. As he did, Jack
got a good look at him.

The man was wearing red leather boots and dirty clothes. Above his right eye, he was missing an eyebrow.

Throwing his back against the outside wall again, Jack stood there, trying not to move. He couldn't believe this was happening to him. Jack opened his eyes wide, willing himself to wake up.

But this wasn't a dream. The man in the cave was none other than Callous Carl, and the men with him were his gang of thieves.

Chapter 9:
The Dilemma

So now Jack knew who he was up against: one of the most dangerous treasure hunters that had ever lived! Jack needed to figure out how to catch these guys and bring them to justice.

He could burst into the cave and try to apprehend them. But his Book Bag didn't contain any gadgets that could overcome five guys at once. His Dozing Spray was only good for two people, and his Tornado only had ropes for binding up to three crooks. Plus, as strong and brave as Jack was, he was only a boy. There was no way he could physically overpower five grown men. It just wasn't going to happen.

Another idea was to call the local authorities. But Jack was in a remote location, and it would take the police a while to get there. Since Callous and his gang were about to move on, it would probably be too late. Making it even more difficult was the fact that Jack didn't know where they were off to. "South" wasn't enough of a lead.

The best thing, Jack figured, was to follow the gang, spy on them and gain more information. He scurried over to a leafy bush and crouched down behind it. Patience was the way to catch these guys, reasoned Jack. Patience, that is, and a lot of luck . . .

Chapter 10:
The Close Call

Just then, Jack heard some movement.
Callous Carl and his gang were leaving
the cave. They began walking out one by
one in a long line with Callous at the
back.

"Hurry up, you losers!" he yelled at his
men. Callous was definitely living up to
his name, thought Jack. He certainly
wasn't a warm and friendly guy.

As they passed by, Jack noticed what

they were carrying. The man in front was carrying the burlap bag of tools. The second was carrying the bottles and the third and fourth had packs strapped to their backs. Callous was carrying nothing but the small bag on his hip.

Jack reasoned that the red stone inside was somehow important to the treasure hunt. Otherwise, Callous wouldn't have bothered to take it from the cave. If Jack could get his hands on the bag or the jewel, he just might be able to stop Callous.

As the men approached the pool of water, one of them turned suddenly and started to march toward Jack! Crouching down, Jack tried to blend into a bush as best he could.

The man reached over him, and grabbed for a white rope that was lying on the other side. As he yanked, an inflatable boat came out of nowhere. It slid over Jack's head and onto the ground. Incredibly, the man hadn't seen Jack, because he carried on lugging the boat until he got to the edge of the water.

There, he placed it in the pool, and one by one the men climbed in. Using some thick sticks as oars, they paddled across the pond to the other side. When they reached it, they pulled the boat out of the

water. Callous took his knife out and slashed a hole in the side of the boat.

"That should stop anybody else from gettin' to the other side easily!" he grunted.

Leaving the remains of the boat behind, the men left the clearing and disappeared from view.

Now it was Jack's turn to make a move. He hurried out from behind the bush and quickly swam across the pond. Dripping when he came out, Jack shook himself off as best as he could. He left the waterfall and the pool behind and made his way down the trail the thieves had taken.

Chapter 11:
The Ride

Keeping a good distance between himself and the gang, Jack tried to listen in on what they were saying.

"What d'ya think we'll find at the next place?" called out one.

"Dunno," said another, "but I'm getting thirsty for gold!"

"Shut your traps!" growled Callous. "I told you to keep your mouths shut. We don't want anyone muscling in on our action."

The men grumbled in agreement.

This little conversation gave Jack an idea. He'd forgotten all about the second clue. If he could somehow get to the next location before Callous and his gang, then he could call the police and capture them before they went any further.

Quietly, Jack pulled out Mr. Garcia's drawing as he walked. The second clue was of a building at the top of a mountain.

As soon as he was in a stationary place, he could use his Double-A device to find the location.

Callous Carl and his gang stepped from the trail and onto the open road. Sticking close behind, Jack hid behind a tree as he watched. There, a few yards away, was a small truck. Hitched to the cab was a small trailer with a tarpaulin on top.

Callous was probably going to try and hide the treasure underneath the tarpaulin and smuggle it back to his headquarters. Jack, however, was thinking of a better, more immediate, use for the hiding place it provided.

As the men were climbing into the truck, Jack made a break for it. He ran from the forest and toward the trailer.

Lifting the tarpaulin, he crawled underneath. Within moments, the truck started up and the trailer began to roll. Callous and his men hadn't seen Jack. Now they were off to the next clue, with Jack going along for the ride.

Chapter 12:
The Next Stop

Although it seemed risky, hiding in the
trailer was Jack's only choice. Since the
Torpedo was in for repairs, Jack didn't have
a gadget that could go more than twenty-
five miles per hour. Besides, Jack would
slip out when the truck slowed down.
Then, he could call the cops as Callous
and his men were at the next location.

In the meantime he had to figure out
where the truck was taking him. He pulled

out Mr. Garcia's drawing of the treasure map and looked hard at the building at the top of a mountain. Given that the Aztecs worshiped many gods, Jack wondered if this was some sort of religious temple.

Not wanting to move the tarpaulin too much, Jack wriggled as little as possible as he reached for his Double-A device. The two As were short for "Archaeology Assistant," and it was a necessary gadget for doing research on the ancient world.

All you had to do was type in a key word or phrase, and the Double-A device would feed back information about what you were looking for. Agents had used it on missions in ancient Greece, and now Jack was going to use it here in Mexico, to find out where they were headed.

After typing the words *temple, mountain,* and *south of Mexico City,* an entry popped up. There was a temple at the top of a mountain called Tepozteco. The mountain was just south of Mexico City.

Jack closed his eyes and allowed himself to nod off. After all, it would be hours before they got to the temple, and Jack needed to conserve his energy for the dangers ahead.

Chapter 13:
The Scare

THWACK!

CRUNCH!

Jack woke up suddenly—his body was being thrown around. The trailer had slowed to a crawl and was now jolting up and down.

Carefully lifting the tarpaulin's flap, Jack peeked out at the view. The truck was on a road in the middle of another forest. But this road wasn't made of tarmac, it was a dirt track, and there were large holes and rocks all over it.

Must be getting close to the temple, thought Jack. Time to slip out of the trailer.

Rolling his body over the back edge of the trailer, Jack let himself fall onto the bumper and then hit the ground.

Jack landed face-first in a muddy hole. Spitting out dirty water, he ran quietly into the bushes. The truck carried on until it came to a stop down the road.

Jack watched as Callous's men hopped out of the vehicle. They walked to the back of the trailer and lifted the cover. For a tense moment Jack wondered if they'd noticed he'd been there, because they stopped dead in their tracks. But then they carried on, taking some equipment and other bags with them.

"Hustle up!" said Callous Carl, stepping out of the truck in his red leather boots. "This is the second stop on the map. If y'all see anybody lurkin'," he said spitting on the ground, "kill 'em. And then ask questions later."

Jack gulped. Callous Carl meant business. He had no doubt that Callous had gotten rid of other people along the way. Now more than ever, it was important to be careful and clever.

The men disappeared into the forest and up a trail to the left. Crouching down,

Jack followed them closely. As the path rose steeply, the men grabbed sticks and vines to keep themselves anchored to the ground. Since Jack was smaller and lighter, all he needed were his hands and feet, which he used to scramble up the hill.

They'd climbed for nearly an hour when at last there was a break in the trees. From below, Jack watched as the men stepped over a ridge. Jack crawled toward it too.

It took him a few moments, but when he reached the top, he peeked over the ridge. There, on the top of the mountain, was a beautiful temple. Because of the difficult climb and its abandoned look, Jack reckoned no one had been there for many years. He saw the last man rush inside the building.

When Jack thought the area was clear,

he made his way over the ridge and onto
flat ground. He found a large boulder, and
perched himself against it.

This was the perfect moment, thought Jack. They were in a remote location and the gang was busy in the temple. All Jack had to do was summon the authorities and then they could surround the temple, trapping the crooks inside.

Pleased with his plan, Jack pushed a few buttons on his Watch Phone, ready to talk.

"*Hola,*" said a voice on the other end. It was the local police station.

"*Hola,*" said Jack, "*Habla inglés?*"

"Yes," said the voice on the other end. "What's your emergency?"

"There are five men," said Jack, "who are trying to steal—"

But before Jack could finish, a large shadow appeared before him. Out of nowhere, a knife swung in front of Jack's eyes and sliced his Watch Phone off his wrist. The gadget sailed into the trees and turned itself off, since it was no longer attached to Jack's arm.

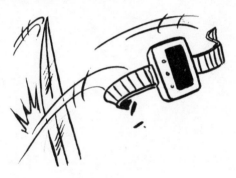

When Jack looked down, he saw red leather boots. He gulped. He knew who it was. It was Callous Carl.

"What do you think you're doing?" the thief growled.

Jack got up and tried to run, but Callous grabbed him by his Book Bag and threw him to the ground.

"Oh, no you don't!" he seethed. "You're gonna pay for coming after me!"

Jack was on his back looking up. Callous held the knife's sharp blade between Jack's eyes. "I'm going to get you piece by piece!"

Jack's heart started to thump. He was finding it hard to breathe. The lack of air was making him dizzy.

"Boss!" yelled a voice in the distance.

Callous's eyes flicked away from Jack.

"Yeah?" He sneered in the direction of the voice. "What d'ya want?"

"We found it!" said the man.

Callous looked down at Jack. "I'm not finished with you, yet," he said. Talking to the man at the temple, he ordered, "Come over here and give me a hand with this kid."

The man rushed over.

"Tie him up!" barked Callous. He bent down close to Jack's face again and looked at him with evil eyes. "I'll come back for you when I'm done," he hissed.

The man did as Callous directed. Using a rope from behind his back, he quickly tied Jack's feet and hands together. Jack didn't dare do a thing. After all, if Jack tried to make a move, he had no doubt Callous would finish him off right then and there.

"That should do ya," grumbled the man. Then he and Callous went back inside the temple.

Chapter 14:
The Way Down

Jack wasn't sure what the men had found, but at this point he didn't much care. The most important thing was to get out of there—and fast.

He stared at his hands and feet. There was no way he could wriggle out of the ties. Hoisting himself into a sitting position, he reached his fingers down to his boots.

Mr. Davidson, the GPF tech wizard, had

stashed a few goodies in every secret agent's shoes. There was the Dome, an expandable bag, under the left sole. A Mine Alert feature was imbedded in the tips. Smoke-Screen Pellets were hidden in the right heel, while a miniature pocket knife was on the side of the left.

It was the last tool Jack was after. He moved his hands over the inside of that shoe and opened a small plastic door. Poking out was the top of the pocket knife. Taking it out, Jack immediately began to cut through the ropes.

Frantically, he looked at the temple doors. The last thing Jack needed was for Callous and his men to come out now. He carried on slicing until the ropes around his hands and his feet broke free.

Putting his knife back in his shoe, Jack quickly ran back to the path. But as soon as he did, he stopped. There was no way he could hike back down that trail. It was steep, and he guessed it would take at least forty-five minutes to descend.

The only other way off the mountain was to abseil. Abseiling was dangerous, and something the GPF recommended only in an emergency. Since Callous had threatened Jack's life and his hooligans were looting treasure, Jack figured this qualified as a critical time.

After pulling his Abseil Kit out of his Book Bag, he anchored the rope, slipped the harness around his waist and placed the Noggin Mold on his head. The floppy piece of rubber instantly hardened to form a protective shell.

Jack raced to the side of the mountain, and turned around with his heels on the edge. He was about to step backward when he heard a noise. It was coming from the temple. Callous and his men had discovered Jack was no longer there.

"The boy!" roared Callous. "He's escaped!"

Quickly, Jack lowered himself over the rim of the mountain, but not soon enough. One of the men noticed Jack's head popping up over the ridge.

"There he is!" he shouted. The men started running toward Jack.

Using his hands and feet as quickly as he could, Jack slid down the rope and the side of the cliff. As he dropped, he looked upward. Callous and his men were now

leaning over the side, watching Jack's every move.

"Get him!" shouted Callous.

ZING!

PING!

Jack ducked. A bullet ricocheted off a rock and into the trees. Only a few more moments and he'd be safe. The voice echoed again from above.

"Cut the rope!" Callous hollered.

Jack figured at least one of the men had a knife handy. He knew he didn't

have much time. Moving quickly, Jack
swung himself far to the right.

WOOSH!

The next thing Jack knew was that he
was falling. One of Callous's thugs had
cut the cord. Crashing into the treetops,
his body bounced from branch to branch
until it fell onto the ground with a thud.

As Jack lay there, he looked through the
leaves. Callous and his men were still
leaning over the ridge, checking that Jack
was toast. He lay completely still to try
and fool them.

From what Jack could see, the gang believed it. They stopped paying attention to Jack and stood up around Carl. Callous pulled something out of the bag on his hip, and as he lifted it to the sun Jack saw something blue sparkle. The gang let out a big cheer, and then Callous put the object away. Jack was pretty sure it was a stone like the one he'd seen at the cave, only this one was obviously a different color. The men congratulated themselves again, and then walked away from the side of the mountain.

Chapter 15:
The Ancient City

Gathering his throbbing body off the ground, Jack hid himself further under the foliage, so that he couldn't be seen. He put away the remnants of his gear and left his Noggin Mold on, just in case.

With no way to alert the authorities now that his Watch Phone was out of action, Jack was going to have to deal with matters himself. Pulling out Mr. Garcia's drawing, Jack took a look at the third and final clue.

The picture was of a triangular building with a crescent-shaped moon on top. It was pretty clear the building was a pyramid, but Jack couldn't figure out the significance of the moon.

Pulling out his Double-A Device, Jack typed the words *pyramid* and *moon*. Hundreds of entries came up, but one in particular caught Jack's eye:

The Pyramid of the Moon is located in the ancient Mexican city of Teotihuacán (say it like tay–o–tee–wah–kan). *Archaeologists have discovered a series of underground tunnels there, although their purpose is still unknown. Approximate distance from present location: 100 miles northwest.*

After reading the description, Jack had a strong hunch it was the right place. The fact that there were a group of underground tunnels pointed to a possibility of buried treasure.

If Jack was right, Callous and his men had already taken what they needed from the temple. Once they'd hiked back down the hill, they'd be off to the pyramid.

Pulling his Flyboard out, Jack snapped it together. He swiped his index finger over the identification grid, and soon the hydrogen jets were up and running. Jack took off northwest, his mind racing with how he would defeat Callous Carl. At least now he would have the element of surprise . . .

Chapter 16:
The Turning Point

Jack had been traveling for a few hours when he arrived at Teotihuacán, the ancient city that had thrived almost a thousand years ago. The ground was drier than it was down south, and there were scrubby bushes sticking out of it. The place seemed deserted, but Jack knew there were thieves lurking about.

Up ahead were several buildings. According to the Double-A device, one was called the Pyramid of the Sun; another was called the Temple of the Feathered Serpent; and at the end of a four-mile long road was the Pyramid of the Moon. Jack and his Flyboard followed the trail to this last temple.

Packing his gadget away, Jack began
to search for clues. To the right of the
building, he saw the back end of a
vehicle. Jack recognized it as Callous's
truck. But there wasn't anybody inside.
Callous and his gang were probably
already under the ground.

Perfect, thought Jack. In the four hours
it took him to travel, Jack had hatched a
new plan, found an old, dusty pay phone
and made an important call. All Jack had
to do now was lure the gang out of the
cave, and his plan to trap them could be
set in motion.

Chapter 17:
The Discovery

Jack found the entrance to the tunnels pretty quickly. Near Callous's truck was a sign sticking out of the dirt with the words KEEP OUT! On the ground next to it was a wooden panel with a handle. When Jack pulled the handle, he found himself staring down a hole in the ground.

Leading downward was a flight of steps. Holding the panel over his head open as long as he could, Jack headed into the depths. When he couldn't keep it open any longer, Jack let the wooden door close. At that moment, everything went dark.

Jack couldn't use his Everglo light, and he'd lost his Watch Phone in the forest. Instead, he used his hands to feel his way around. Counting the steps, Jack noticed there were twenty steps until he hit flat ground again. This must be the beginning of the tunnel, he thought, as he continued to move forward, trying to keep track of whether he was turning left or right. Eventually, up ahead, he could see a faint light. Figuring it was the treasure hunters, Jack made his way toward it.

As the light grew brighter, Jack could see what was up ahead. He was still in a long corridor, but the tunnel was opening into a large room. This room led to another, and so on and so on, until there was only one room left in the cavern.

It was in this last room that Jack found Callous and his band of thieves. They were staring at a painting on the back wall. The only light in the room was from an electric lantern, which was in the middle of the floor. Jack kept himself hidden in the doorway, so that he didn't announce his presence too soon.

The painting was of a man dressed in feathers. Recognizing the image immediately, Jack shuddered. It was of Quetzalcoatl—the feathered serpent—one of the most feared gods of the Aztec people.

But there was something odd about the figure. Whoever had painted it had left small round holes for the god's eyes. Seeing this made Jack think about the stones Callous had collected from the cave and the temple on the mountain. They looked to be the same size and shape as the eyes on the Aztec god.

Maybe, Jack reasoned, the first two clues on the map were about collecting the jewels. The third was about the place where you had to use them. Perhaps, Jack thought, if you placed the stones in the feathered serpent's eyes, it would reveal the location of the buried treasure.

Callous must have had the same thought too, because at that very moment he took the small bag from his hip. He reached inside and pulled out the blue stone. Lifting it to the wall, Callous stuck the jewel into one of the eyes. When he did, the wall swung forward a bit, revealing a secret chamber behind. From where Jack was standing, he could see something gold inside, sparkling in the light.

"The treasure's ours!" shouted Callous.

"Yahoo!" screamed the men, who were drooling and rubbing their hands.

Callous lifted the bag again. He was going to place the last stone in the wall when Jack decided to make a move.

Swooping in, Jack kicked the lantern across the floor, breaking it into pieces. Everything went completely black.

"What's happening?" screamed Callous

Carl. "What the heck happened to our light?"

Remembering where Callous was standing, Jack snatched the bag containing the red stone out of his hands. He turned and ran out of the room and into the tunnel.

"Somebody's stolen the bag!" yelled Callous. "Go after it!" he ordered his men.

Jack could hear the men fumbling around in the dark. Swiping his hands against the tunnel wall as he ran, Jack made sure he didn't crash into anything.

"Get him!" yelled Callous. "Turn another light on!" he screamed.

Jack kept racing toward the exit. He had to lure Callous's men out of the cave.

A light turned on behind Jack, but it wasn't soon enough. His foot jammed into the first step of the stairway and the bag flew out of his hands. Scurrying around, he found it again and started climbing the steps two at a time. The men were now entering the first room.

Reaching the top of the stairs, Jack flung the door open. Light poured into the cave. He dashed out and onto the ground. Jack looked around. But nobody was there.

Jack yelled out in frustration. He could hear Callous's goons stomping up the steps. In the distance, he noticed a small town. His only choice was to lead them there.

Sprinting as fast as he could, Jack headed onto the open plains. The men behind him were shouting vicious threats. They were slowly catching up to Jack.

In front of Jack was a prickly bush. Throwing his body over it, his feet came crashing to the ground. The men did the same. Jack could hear them grunt as they landed.

The next thing he knew, he heard the wheels of a car to his side. It sounded like it was churning up dirt. Thinking help had arrived, Jack was horrified to see that it was Callous driving the truck, with his gang of thieves just behind.

Then, out of nowhere, Jack tripped. He

fell forward to the ground, crashing onto his hands. Jack couldn't help but remember his nightmare. The events of it were exactly what was happening now.

The shadows of the men were closing in on Jack. As they reached for him, Jack screamed "No!"

Just then, Jack heard a horrible screeching sound. He wondered if Callous's car was out of control and headed for him. Jack looked toward the noise.

Speeding toward Jack were ten Mexican police cars, their sirens blaring loudly.

As soon as they saw the police, the men backed away from Jack. They started to run toward Callous and his truck, trying to flee the scene before being captured.

Callous slowed down to let the men climb in, but in doing so lost valuable

time. Nine of the police cars circled around the truck and surrounded the men. There was no way they could escape now.

The last car made its way over to Jack. It braked hard, sending dust spiraling into Jack's face. A Mexican officer hopped out. Knowing Jack was English, he spoke to him in his own language.

"Jack," he said, "I'm sorry we were late. I'd like to blame it on traffic," he added, smiling sheepishly, "but it's siesta time and I had a hard time waking my guys."

Jack shook his head. He didn't know whether to laugh or be angry.

"That's okay," said Jack. "In the end, you saved the day."

"No," said the officer. "It looks like *you* did. Callous Carl has been on the Most Wanted list for years. He's been terrorizing people and stealing treasure for as long as anybody can remember. With him locked up," he added, "Mexico will be a safer place."

Jack stood up and brushed the dust off his clothes. He handed the bag with the remaining stone to the officer.

"This needs to be protected," he said. "If you keep it safe, nobody will be able to steal Montezuma's gold."

"I'll hand it over to the proper authorities in Mexico City." said the officer.

"You'll also need to seal the site," said
Jack, "to make sure nobody else tries to
take anything from there."

"Already done," said the officer, "I've
sent some of my best men over to cover
it."

"Two more things," said Jack. "When you
search Callous, you'll find a map. When
you do," he explained, "you need to return
it to Mr. Garcia. This is his address." Jack
wrote it down on a piece of paper and
gave it to the man. "Tell him he needs to
put it in a safer place from now on." Jack
smiled.

Jack could tell the officer didn't completely understand, but he would probably do as Jack asked.

"Did you run a check on Maria, Mr.
Garcia's cleaner?" asked Jack.

"Sure did," said the officer. "That was a good hunch you had. One of Callous's men is related to her, which is how they knew about the map. We're sending officers to her house right now," he explained, "to pick her up and bring her in for questioning."

"Great," said Jack, who was pleased with how things were turning out.

As he looked over at Callous Carl, he couldn't help but smile. He was being dragged out of the truck, tossed to the ground and cuffed alongside his thugs. When the officers yanked Carl to his feet, the treasure hunter glared in Jack's direction.

"I'm going to get you," he mouthed to him.

"No, you won't," Jack mouthed back.

Carl growled, and then the officers shoved him and his goons into the back

of one of the squad cars. As the car drove
away, Jack waved. It would be a long time
before anyone saw Callous Carl again.

Chapter 18:
The Resolution

With everything sorting itself out, it was time for Jack to go. But, without his Watch Phone, he couldn't very well command it to transport him home.

He waited for the police to leave the scene and when he was sure everyone was gone, he opened his Book Bag. He pulled out his portable Magic Map and laid it on the ground. Whenever a secret agent was away from home, they could use this map and a piece from Whizzy to transport them to their mission.

But because Jack was trying to make the reverse happen, he had to do a very different thing. He placed his first finger over the country of England and counted to five. When it registered his fingerprint and his home destination, a light began to shine from within the country.

When it did, Jack yelled, "Off to England!" and the light burst, swallowing Jack into the map.

When he arrived, he found both he and his map standing in the middle of his room. He folded up his portable map and tucked his Book Bag back under his bed. Accessing the GPF secure site on his computer, he sent them an e-mail telling them of the mishap with his Watch Phone and asking for a new one. Then, he returned to his bed and opened his book about treasure hunters.

He flipped to the story about Callous Carl, and looked at the snarling face of that greedy man. Ripping the pages from his book, Jack crumpled them up and threw them in the wastebasket.

Callous Carl no longer existed, as far as Jack was concerned. Thanks to Jack, Carl was off the Most Wanted list. Carl was about to spend his days cleaning toilets, serving meals and washing clothes in a high-security prison. And that, thought Jack, was exactly where he deserved to be.

The Theft of the
Samurai Sword:
JAPAN

BOOK (11)

The Theft of the Samurai Sword:
JAPAN

Elizabeth Singer Hunt

Illustrated by Brian Williamson

WEINSTEIN BOOKS

For Max, Eve, Doug and Hilary

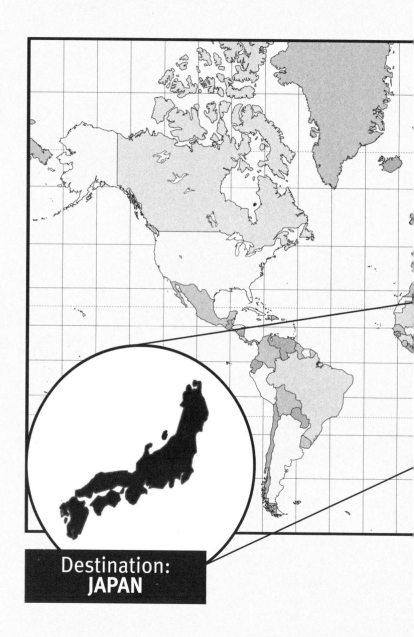

Destination:
JAPAN

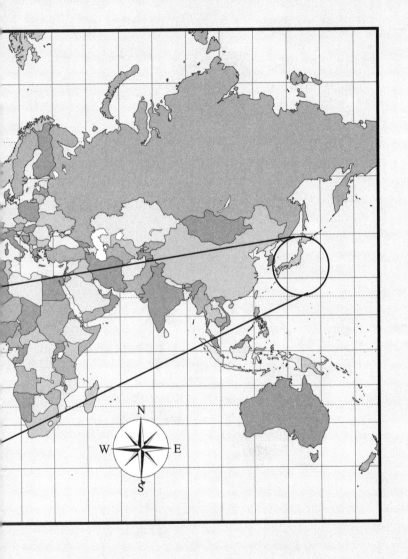

GLOBAL PROTECTION FORCE FILE ON
JACK STALWART

Jack Stalwart applied to be a secret
agent for the Global Protection
Force four months ago.

My name is Jack Stalwart. My older brother,

Max, was a secret agent for you, until he

disappeared on one of your missions. Now I

want to be a secret agent too. If you choose

me, I will be an excellent secret agent and get

rid of evil villains, just like my brother did.

Sincerely,

Jack Stalwart

THINGS YOU'LL FIND IN EVERY BOOK

Watch Phone: The only gadget Jack wears all the time, even when he's not on official business. His Watch Phone is the central gadget that makes most others work. There are lots of important features, most importantly the "C" button, which reveals the code of the day—necessary to unlock Jack's Secret Agent Book Bag. There are buttons on both sides, one of which ejects his life-saving Melting Ink Pen. Beyond these functions, it also works as a phone and, of course, gives Jack the time of day.

Global Protection Force (GPF): The GPF is the organization Jack works for. It's a worldwide force of young secret agents whose aim is to protect the world's people, places and possessions. No one knows exactly where its main offices are located (all correspondence and gadgets for repair are sent to a special P.O. Box, and training is held at various locations around the world), but Jack thinks it's somewhere cold, like the Arctic Circle.

Whizzy: Jack's magical miniature globe. Almost every night at precisely 7:30 P.M., the GPF uses Whizzy to send Jack the identity of the country that he must travel to. Whizzy can't talk, but he can cough up messages. Jack's parents don't know Whizzy is anything more than a normal globe.

The Magic Map: The magical map hanging on Jack's bedroom wall. Unlike most maps, the GPF's map is made of a mysterious wood. Once Jack inserts the country piece from Whizzy, the map swallows Jack whole and sends him away on his missions. When he returns, he arrives precisely one minute after he left.

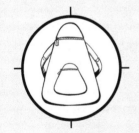

Secret Agent Book Bag: The Book Bag that Jack wears on every adventure. Licensed only to GPF secret agents, it contains top-secret gadgets necessary to foil bad guys and escape certain death. To activate the bag before each mission, Jack must punch in a secret code given to him by his Watch Phone. Once he's away, all he has to do is place his finger on the zip, which identifies him as the owner of the bag and immediately opens.

THE STALWART FAMILY

Jack's dad, John

He moved the family to England when Jack was two, in order to take a job with an aerospace company. Jack's dad thinks he is an ordinary boy and that his other son, Max, attends a school in Switzerland. Jack's dad is American and his mum is British, which makes Jack a bit of both.

Jack's mum, Corinne

One of the greatest mums as far as Jack is concerned. When she and her husband received a letter from a posh school in Switzerland inviting Max to attend, they were overjoyed. Since Max left six months ago, they have received numerous notes in Max's handwriting telling them he's OK. Little do they know it's all a lie and that it's the GPF sending those letters.

Jack's older brother, Max

Two years ago, at the age of nine, Max joined the GPF. Max used to tell Jack about his adventures and show him how to work his secret-agent gadgets. When the family received a letter inviting Max to attend a school in Europe, Jack figured it was to do with the GPF. Max told him he was right, but that he couldn't tell Jack anything about why he was going away.

Nine-year-old Jack Stalwart

Four months ago, Jack received an anonymous note saying: "Your brother is in danger. Only you can save him." As soon as he could, Jack applied to be a secret agent too. Since that time, he's battled some of the world's most dangerous villains, and hopes some day in his travels to find and rescue his brother, Max.

DESTINATION:
Japan

The tallest mountain in Japan is called Mount Fuji. It is 12,388 feet tall.

□

The Japanese flag is white with a red circle in the middle, symbolizing the rising sun.

□

The Japanese name for Japan is Nippon.

□

Over 127 million people live in Japan.

The capital city of Japan is Tokyo.

□

Japan's currency is the yen.

The Great Travel Guide

GPF Culture Guide: Japan
Eating and Karaoke

One of the most popular foods in Japan—
and around the world—is sushi.

Most people think of sushi as being fish and
rice wrapped in pressed sheets of seaweed.
But it can also be a bowl of rice topped with
fish, meat or vegetables.

Japanese people use chopsticks to eat
their food.

Karaoke—singing into a microphone while
reading lyrics to a song on a video screen—
started in Japan.

GPF FAST FACTS: THE SAMURAI

The word "samurai" means
"those who serve."

They were the warriors of Japan until
the late 1800s.

In later years they won so many battles
and gained so much power that
they ruled Japan.

The word "bushido" means "way of the
warrior" and refers to the code of
conduct the samurai lived by.

The samurai used many weapons including
swords, bows, daggers and spears.
The most famous of all is
called a "katana."

If you were born into a samurai family,
you received a sword when you turned
thirteen years old.

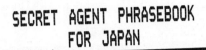

SECRET AGENT PHRASEBOOK FOR JAPAN

SECRET AGENT GADGET INSTRUCTION MANUAL

Antidote Pack: If you suspect that you've been poisoned, use the GPF's Antidote Pack to save your life. Figure out which part of your body is being affected and place the right vial in the syringe. Each vial is marked with the name of a body system: Cardiovascular, Immune, Muscular, Nervous, Respiratory, Skeletal. Jab the needle into the upper part of your bottom, and release the serum. It could take as long as fifteen minutes to work.

Scatta-Scooter: When you need to travel faster than your feet will take you, use the GPF's Scatta-Scooter. It looks like an ordinary scooter, but has a battery-powered engine fixed to the back. To re-charge, simply plug it in for one hour.

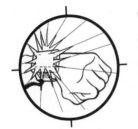

"Flash" on Watch Phone:
Effective today, all Watch Phones will be updated to include a "flash" feature. With it, an agent can send a high-powered flash of light in short bursts. Perfect if you need to temporarily blind someone, or to send a rescue signal if you're lost at sea.

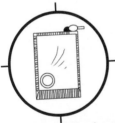

Wax Statue Dust:
The GPF's Wax Statue Dust can freeze someone stiff for a period of one hour. Just sprinkle it over a person's head and within moments that person's skin and muscles will be completely still. Their insides however will remain fully functional.

Chapter 1:
The Madame

It was a hot summer night in a far away
country. A large lady wearing lots of
makeup and a pretty kimono was sitting
on top of a chair in the middle of a room.
Her ruby-red lips parted, and she spoke
to the four men standing before her. The
men were dressed in black from head to
toe. Hanging from their cheeks were black
veils. The only thing you could see was
their piercing dark eyes.

"OK, men," she said. "You've heard your instructions. Now go and claim my treasures."

The men bowed and shouted the word "hai" together. They held onto their batons, which were fixed to their sides, and then turned and ran out of the room.

Throwing her head back, the woman cackled with evil laughter. The glittery green powder that covered her eyelids sparkled in the light. As she brought her head forward, she smiled with smug satisfaction.

Now all Madame Midori had to do was sit back and relax. Within hours, her band of ninja thieves would return, bringing with them the treasures she so desperately wanted.

Chapter 2:
The First Ninja

Within moments of leaving Madame Midori, ninja number one was hot on the job. He ran through the streets like a shadow, hopping over garbage cans, surfing around cars and sneaking through parks and gardens.

Up ahead, he spied a two story house with a red tiled roof. The house was surrounded by a high stone wall. This was the home of Mr. Taka, ninja number one's target.

Mr. Taka was a very wealthy businessman. He'd amassed so much money that he'd started to buy priceless works of art. Mr. Taka's private art collection was known throughout the world as one of the best. Because of this, some of his valuables were kept in a locked safe in his house.

Luckily for ninja number one, Madame Midori had done some work ahead of time. She'd obtained the layout of Mr. Taka's home (purchased for a large sum from the previous owner). She'd also given him an electronic code breaker (bought from an unsavory character in the warehouse district).

Now all he had to do was get inside, and use his speed and skill to steal one particular object for Madame Midori.

He scaled the stone wall and jumped down to the garden below. Crouching low, he ran toward the house. Stopping underneath an open window on the second floor, he looked around the grounds to make sure no security was patroling. From the map Madame Midori had given him, ninja number one knew that the open window led to Mr. Taka's bedroom.

Satisfied that he was alone, ninja

number one shot a long nylon rope outward from his hip. Attached to it was a metal claw. He waited for it to stick its teeth into the wooden window frame, and yanked on it to make sure it was stuck.

As he crawled over the window ledge and into Mr. Taka's house, he grinned. Success would soon be his.

Chapter 3:
The First Theft

Ninja number one was part of a four-man team hired by Madame Midori. They were asked to pull off one of the trickiest thefts in Japan's history—stealing four national treasures at the same time. While ninja number one was focused on Mr. Taka's house, the other men were scattered across Tokyo stealing priceless objects too.

Madame Midori called these men her

"ninjas" because they were trained in martial arts and practiced the "art of stealth." For most people, being involved in something like this would lead to a feeling of shame and guilt. But the only thing ninja number one could think about was the money Madame Midori promised to put into his bank account when the task was done.

As he stepped onto Mr. Taka's floor, he immediately looked to the bed. Mr. Taka was snoring like a bulldozer while Mrs. Taka slept peacefully by his side. Ninja number one shook his head in amazement. How someone could sleep so well next to something that noisy was beyond belief.

Thanks to a small nightlight plugged into the wall, ninja number one could see everything in the bedroom. Creeping like a cat, the thief walked over to a framed painting of a smirking woman dressed in brown.

Although it looked similar, he knew the real *Mona Lisa* hung in a museum in Paris. Madame Midori had bribed an old housekeeper to tell her where Mr. Taka's locked safe was. It was cleverly hidden behind this fake painting on the wall.

Sure enough, as he slid the framed painting to the left, it revealed an electronic safe. He hooked his code breaker over the keypad and within moments it had retrieved Mr. Taka's secret code. The safe was soon deactivated and the door to it popped open with a click.

At the noise, ninja number one glanced in Mr. Taka's direction. The man snorted and snuffled, and then went back to dozing noisily again.

The thief opened the safe and looked

inside. There, lying on its side and deep into the wall, was what he was searching for. He removed it from its hiding place, and took a good look.

Its long wooden sheath was painted black. Decorating its gold handle were stones and expensive leathers. The curved steel blade inside glistened in the light when he pulled it out of its sheath.

Although he felt no guilt in taking it, ninja number one felt awe at holding an ancient samurai sword that was over 600 years old.

Just then, Mr. Taka sat up in his bed. Ninja number one froze, nearly dropping the sword in fright. Mr. Taka twisted his body around, so that he was facing his bedside table. Reaching out, he grabbed a glass of water and drank it down. When he was finished, he crawled back under the covers and closed his eyes. Within moments Mr. Taka was snoring again.

Relieved, ninja number one stashed the sword into a bag that was strapped to his back. He closed the safe door and pushed the REACTIVATE button on his code breaker. Once the door locked again, he silently slid the fake *Mona Lisa* back into place.

All he had to do now was get out of there without being seen. He dashed to the window and stepped onto the ledge. Grabbing the rope, he swung down from the window and landed on the ground. As he yanked the metal claw from the window ledge, it made a sharp pinging noise.

The main light in Mr. Taka's bedroom window flickered on. Ninja number one could hear voices inside. The noise of the claw had woken them up.

Standing still, he was horrified to see Mrs. Taka peer from the window. She was looking outside for the source of the sound. Ninja number one tried to hide, but another light flickered on from a downstairs room. The only thing he could do was try to escape. He sprinted across the grounds and toward the stone wall.

Throwing his hands up, he climbed as

fast as he could up and over the stones. As he got to the ledge, he took a quick look in the direction of the house. Mrs. Taka was running around frantically, screaming. She'd seen the veiled intruder moving speedily across their grounds.

Ninja number one jumped to the other side of the wall, but not before a piece of paper fell from his pocket. Unfortunately for him, he didn't realize it until he was nearly back at Madame Midori's. By then, it was too late to turn back.

Chapter 4:
The Warrior

At around the same time, but thousands
of miles away, Jack Stalwart was sitting at
his bedroom desk reading a book he'd
checked out at the local library. It was
called *The Samurai*.

The samurai were legendary fighters in
Japan. They used to work for the lords
and emperor, until they gained so much
power that they ended up ruling the
country themselves. The samurai (led by a

shogun) ruled Japan for nearly six hundred years. In 1868 the last shogun gave up his power and Japan was ruled by an emperor again.

Jack flicked through the book and looked at a drawing of the samurai's armor. He was always fascinated by a warrior's dress. Samurai wore a helmet, shoulder and breast plates and guards for their arms, shins and thighs.

Although samurai used bow and arrows and spears, the *katana* was the most famous of all samurai weapons. It was a long, sharp sword. The picture in Jack's book was of a fifteenth century katana that belonged to a great samurai ruler.

At about the same time that Jack finished his book, he heard a sound coming from his bedside table. It was Whizzy, his magical miniature globe. Whizzy was starting to spin.

Besides Jack's Watch Phone and the secure website link, Whizzy was Jack's only connection with the GPF. It was through

Whizzy that the GPF gave Jack the location of his next mission.

Jack was a secret agent for the Global Protection Force. The GPF was a worldwide force of secret agents responsible for protecting the world's most precious treasures. "Protect that which cannot protect itself" was the motto of the GPF, and the code of honor that Jack and the other agents lived by.

He joined the force several months ago, when his brother Max (also an agent with the GPF) disappeared on one of their missions. Since then, he'd been gathering clues about his brother's whereabouts.

Until there was a break in that case, Jack had to fulfill his other secret agent duties. To that end, he turned his attention back to Whizzy who was spinning furiously.

Jack rushed over to his tiny globe. As he watched Whizzy twirl, he waited for him to do his thing. Whizzy coughed—

Ahem! A collection of small jigsaw pieces blew out of his mouth and onto the floor.

When he saw how many bits there were, Jack figured he was going to an island chain. He picked up the pieces, and carried them over to his Magic Map.

As he looked at the map that covered his wall, Jack tried to figure out where his mission could be. There was Indonesia, but that had more islands than Jack had in his hand. There was New Zealand but the shape of the country didn't fit. Finally, he looked at Japan. One by one, Jack placed the pieces in the right places.

Soon, the name Japan flashed from within that country and then disappeared again. Rushing over to his bed, Jack pulled his Book Bag out from underneath. He asked his Watch Phone for the code of the day. When he received the word SUSHI, he tapped it into his Book Bag's lock.

Instantly, the bag popped open. He checked to make sure everything was there. Jack noticed that several new gadgets—the Antidote Pack and Wax Statue Dust—had been added to his bag. He'd read about them in the latest GPF Gadget Instruction Manual. Excitedly, Jack locked his Book Bag again. Then he rushed back to the Magic Map.

The light inside Japan was glowing brightly now, illuminating his entire room.

When Jack was ready, he yelled "Off to Japan!" and with that command, the light burst, swallowing him inside his Magic Map.

Chapter 5:
The Commander

When Jack arrived, he found himself on a path next to a rectangular area filled with sand. Dotted throughout the sand were large rocks. Around the rocks, someone had raked the sand in circles.

As Jack looked at it, he realized that the sand looked like water, and the rocks looked like islands. Wondering whether this was arranged to look like the islands of Japan itself, Jack let his eyes scan his

surroundings. Elsewhere there were some maple trees and bamboo. There were also some stone Japanese lanterns dotted throughout.

Around the garden was a stone wall, and in front of him was a two story house. There were red tiles on the roof and a red door at the front. He walked up to the door and knocked. He figured his contact was on the other side.

A man answered. He was tall and thin and dressed in a smart suit. Jack waited for him to say something first.

"Hello," the man said in English. "They're waiting for you upstairs."

Jack was confused. Who were "they" and who was this man? Plus, how did he know to speak to Jack in English?

Jack stepped cautiously into the house. Spying some slippers on a step on the floor, Jack removed his boots and tucked them into his Book Bag.

Although it was customary to take off your shoes in a Japanese house, Jack didn't feel like leaving his life-saving GPF boots behind. After all, there were at least four gadgets tucked on the sides and in the soles of his boots.

"Follow me," said the man once Jack had put on the slippers. Jack did as he was told. He followed the man—who he guessed must be a butler—down a long hallway and past several rooms. The rooms had beige-colored woven mats on the floor, and paper and wood doors that slid open.

They climbed some stairs at the end of the hall and entered a room full of Japanese policemen who also weren't wearing shoes. The butler left Jack, and returned to his duties downstairs.

Jack counted at least ten men. He gulped at the thought of why so many policemen were gathered in somebody's house.

"Konnichiwa," said Jack, saying "hello" in Japanese.

The men bowed and then moved apart, revealing another, more senior-looking man. Jack could tell he was more important, not only by the way the other men acted around him, but also by what he was wearing.

This man was taller than the rest, and had a crisp, white shirt tucked underneath a dark jacket and pants. He was also wearing a dark tie.

"Hello," he said, as he bowed his head.

"We are so honored that you could come to help us."

Jack bowed back to the man, wanting to make sure he showed due respect.

"I am Superintendent General Ito," the man continued. "Chief of the Tokyo Police."

Wow, Jack thought quietly to himself. Whatever happened here must have been serious. The boss of such a prestigious police force didn't show up unless the crime was really important.

"Tonight," said the chief, "Japan has suffered a terrible series of crimes."

"What's happened?" asked Jack.

The chief shook his head. "No less than four priceless Japanese treasures were stolen from museums and private collections across Tokyo." He paused. "All within half an hour of each other."

"All at nearly the same time?" asked Jack. He couldn't believe one crook could pull off such an amazing feat.

"Yes," Chief Ito said, "unbelievable, right? We're thinking it was done by a team of thieves."

"That would make sense," said Jack. "What did they take?"

"They took a beautiful antique kimono from the Museum of Tokyo," the police chief replied. "It was over five hundred years old and was used in a Noh play."

Jack knew that kimonos were a kind of robe worn by Japanese people. "Noh" was a classic Japanese play acted out mostly by men.

"Also from the Tokyo Museum," Chief Ito added, "they stole a painting by Sesshū Tōyō, one of the most famous Japanese painters. From a Mrs. Sato they stole a priceless strand of cultured pearls." Cultured pearls were perfectly round, and the process of making them was patented by a Japanese man in the early 1900s. "And finally," he added, "they stole an ancient samurai sword from the man who lives in this house. Here's a picture of Mr. Taka's sword."

The chief showed Jack a color photograph.

"I know this sword," said Jack. "It's from the fifteenth century, right?" Jack couldn't help but be shocked at the coincidence. This was the sword in his library book at home.

"Yes," said the chief. "From what I understand, it was used by one of the most powerful samurai over six hundred years ago. It is truly priceless."

"Do you mind if I ask Mr. Taka some questions?" asked Jack. While he had no doubt the boss of the Tokyo police force had been thorough, he wanted to interview the owner of the sword himself.

Chief Ito nodded and motioned for Jack to enter another room.

Chapter 6:
The Sobbing Man

Jack went into Mr. Taka's bedroom and found the man sitting on the edge of his bed. He was still in his pajamas, and was sobbing uncontrollably into his hands. His dutiful wife was trying to comfort him.

"Konnichiwa," Jack said gently to the man.

Mr. Taka stopped crying for the moment and looked up at Jack. His face was red and wet with tears.

"I understand your sword was stolen in the middle of the night," said Jack.

The man nodded "yes."

"Was anything else taken?" asked Jack.

The man shook his head "no."

"Did you hear or see anything suspicious?" asked Jack.

Mr. Taka's wife piped up. "I saw a dark shadow running across our garden and toward the wall," she said. "He jumped over it and ran away with our sword."

Hearing this reminder, Mr. Taka started sobbing all over again.

Jack left them alone and walked up to Chief Ito.

"Have you checked the grounds?" Jack asked.

"Yes," he replied. "One of the first things we did after fingerprinting the room. There was nothing there, nor anything in the house. It's the same at each of the four crime scenes. The crooks left nothing behind."

Jack didn't necessarily believe that. There was always some sort of clue to be found. With the focus of the detective work going on inside Mr. Taka's bedroom, Jack decided to take a look outside.

"Do you mind if I examine the grounds?" asked Jack.

"By all means," said the the chief. "We're finished up there. If you find

35

anything come back and tell me, or give me a call."

He handed Jack his business card with his contact details.

"I understand from the GPF that you're used to working on your own," he said. "I hope you can appreciate that I can't give you any of my men. The entire Tokyo police force is spread thin across the city, interviewing people and trying to solve these crimes."

"No problem," said Jack. "I understand you have your hands full."

Chief Ito turned away from Jack and took an urgent call on his cell phone. Jack made his way down the stairs, and changed out of the slippers and back into his boots. It was time to get to work.

Chapter 7:
The Lead

Jack left the house, walked into the garden, and stood under Mr. Taka's open bedroom window. From below, Jack could see the teeth marks made by the claw that had lifted the crook into Mr. Taka's house.

There were a few messy footprints on the ground below the window, but nothing more to give Jack any clues. He traced the path from the window to the wall. When he got to the wall, he looked around. There were no obvious clues there either.

Since the thief escaped by climbing the wall Jack decided to follow in his footsteps. He crossed over the sand and stone area, climbed the wall, and perched himself at the top. From there, he could see Mr. Taka's bedroom window.

For a moment, Jack made himself think as if he were the thief. He wondered whether the burglar grew nervous when Mrs. Taka saw him at the wall. Jack looked to the ground on the other side. But there was nothing there. Maybe the Chief was right. Perhaps, Jack thought, the thief hadn't left any clues.

Just as Jack was about to climb down, he spied a white piece of paper resting on the top of the wall. He reached over to pick it up. Opening it, Jack tried to make sense of the Japanese characters scribbled on the note. But he wasn't able to read Japanese.

He pulled out his Secret Language Decoder and scanned the gadget from right to left over the writing. (In Japan everything was written from right to left.)

Within moments, Jack's gadget had translated the scribble into a language that Jack could understand. The middle of the screen said:

THE GOLDEN DUCK

Jack couldn't be sure that this piece of paper had been left by the thief, but it was all he had to go on. He picked up his Watch Phone and called Chief Ito. When he picked up, Jack told him about the note. He asked whether the police chief knew what "The Golden Duck" meant.

"Well," he said, "I'm not sure. There's a karaoke club called The Golden Duck in Tokyo. Maybe it refers to that place."

"I'll check it out," said Jack. "This could lead us to more information about the team that committed these crimes."

"You do that," said Chief Ito. "Let me know what you find out."

"Will do," said Jack, as he signed off.

Chapter 8:
The Route

The next thing Jack did was pull out his Map Mate. Every GPF agent was given one of these clever, handheld devices. It could tell you how to get from point A to B using arrows. It did this thanks to satellites in space that fed information into the device.

He input the name "The Golden Duck" and told it to search the city of Tokyo.

Within seconds, his Map Mate had calculated his route.

According to his gadget, it would take about an hour to get there by foot. Jack didn't need the power of his Flyboard, so he pulled out something that was less robust. It was called the Scatta-Scooter.

The GPF's Scatta-Scooter looked like an ordinary scooter, but it had a battery-powered engine attached to the back. It wasn't as fast as the Flyboard—it could only do up to fifteen miles per hour. But for a job like this, where he didn't want to draw too much attention to himself, it was perfect.

Snapping it together, Jack hopped on. He put on his Noggin Mold, hooked his Map Mate to the handlebars and took off.

Chapter 9:
The Club

Jack cruised from the residential areas around Tokyo and into the main city itself. This was the capital city of Japan. As far as Jack was concerned, it was one of the most exciting cities he'd ever seen.

There were neon lights all around and music coming from the shops. People were bustling everywhere. There were stores selling funky clothes, music devices and even robotic dogs. He cruised

by a restaurant selling sushi rolls, or rice
and avocado wrapped inside seaweed.

The red light on the Map Mate was
blinking, which told Jack he was close. He
slowed down his Scatta-Scooter, turned it
off and packed it away.

He walked over to a glittering door with
an awning over it. There was a sign on it,
written in English for the tourists.

The Golden Duck
Tokyo's Most Famous Karaoke Club
Open 24 hours
Come inside

This was it. This was the name on the paper. Jack did what the sign said and entered the club. As soon as he did, he was overwhelmed by noise.

It was lunchtime, and The Golden Duck was really buzzing. There was a main stage in the middle of the room. A TV screen hung from the ceiling to the left. On the screen were words to songs written in both Japanese and English.

Jack knew exactly what this was about. His buddy Richard had introduced him to the idea of karaoke back home in England. When Richard turned eight, his Mum had bought him a karaoke machine. Since then, Jack, Charlie and Richard had spent hours singing old songs from when their parents were young.

All you had to do was sing to the words on the TV screen. If you did it right, you'd sound just like the people that created

the song in the first place. It was a fantastically fun thing to do. And it had been created right here in Japan.

An older man dressed in a suit made his way to the stage. He stood in front of the microphone, and the music started to play. It was the song "Summer Nights" from the 1978 movie *Grease*.

The man wiped the sweat off his brow and began to sing. Although he was trying his best, Jack couldn't help but think the man sounded like a strangled chicken.

Making his way across the room, Jack walked over to a man making drinks at the bar. He asked the man where he could find the owner of the club.

"There she is," he said, pointing to a large woman. The older man had finished his song, and this woman was stepping onto the stage.

"That's Madame Midori," he said. "One

of the best karaoke entertainers in all of Tokyo."

She grabbed the microphone as another song came on. It was "I Will Survive" by a lady named Gloria Gaynor. Jack had heard his Mum sing it around their house. Madame Midori began to belt out the tune. As she sang, Jack couldn't believe how good it sounded. The green eye shadow on her lids glistened in the light of the disco ball overhead.

When she finished, the crowd went wild. She lapped up their applause and then spoke into the microphone in English.

"Thank you all for coming," she said. Then she waved to the audience and left the stage.

Chapter 10:
The Fateful Meeting

Jack caught up with the woman as she was walking away.

"Madame Midori," he said. "I'd love to speak with you."

The woman pulled a pen from her pocket and lifted it toward Jack.

"Where do you want me to sign?" she asked.

"Huh?" said Jack. He was a bit confused.

"You want my autograph, right?" she said.

"Oh, yes," Jack said, not wanting to offend her. He scraped together a bit of paper from his trouser pocket and handed it to her.

"What do you want me to say?" she asked.

"Maybe 'To Jack, from Madame Midori,'" he said.

"Very well then," she said as she scribbled.

"Could I ask you a few questions?" asked Jack.

"Sure," she said.

"A piece of paper with your club's name on it was found at the scene of a major theft last night," said Jack.

At that, Madame Midori stopped signing her name.

"What do you mean?" she said, quickly and sharply.

"I've been asked by the chief of the

Tokyo Police to follow up a lead," offered Jack. "It seems that a crook who stole an antique samurai sword last night had the name of your club on a piece of paper he carried with him."

Madame Midori looked gravely at Jack. "That's very odd news," she said. "I can't imagine why."

"Well," said Jack. "Maybe he worked here. Can you think of anyone that you've hired recently that could be a suspect?"

"No," she said, starting to shift away from Jack.

"Well," Jack pressed on, "is there anyone you can think of who's visited your club recently that may have committed a crime like this?"

"None that I can think of," Madame Midori said. She paused for a moment, and then her eyes lightened again.

"You know," she said. "It's very noisy in here. I think it might be best if we talk in a quieter place. You're obviously visiting from out of town, why don't you meet me at my home? Then we can talk things through."

Jack thought it was a good idea. It was definitely noisy here in the club.

"OK," he said.

"Here's the address," said Madame Midori. She handed Jack a card with an address written in English and Japanese.

"Why don't we meet there in, say, fifteen minutes," she said.

"Great," said Jack. He figured the time would give him the chance to collect his thoughts and prepare a more thorough list of questions.

Jack said goodbye to Madame Midori, who soon vanished to somewhere else in the club.

He stepped outside and caught a breath of fresh air. Programming his Map Mate for Madame Midori's home, he saw that it would take only ten minutes to get there. That meant he had a few more minutes to kill.

Across the road, he spied a vendor selling lunch. He crossed over and bought himself a squid steak on a stick.

Delicious, he thought, as he bit into the grilled white meat. He'd never tasted anything quite like this before.

Chapter 11:
The Decision

Madame Midori fumed as she left. How on earth did that pip-squeak find out where she was? It must have been that idiot, ninja number one, dropping that piece of paper. This wasn't the first time he'd done something stupid. She'd deal with him and his clumsiness later.

For now, she had to focus on that kid. She needed to figure out a way to throw him off her trail, or better yet get rid of him altogether.

Soon, an idea popped into her mind. Madame Midori hurried to her car and climbed onto the driver's seat. Fumbling through her handbag, she pulled out her cell phone. Punching the buttons, she made two quick phone calls. One was to a local fish-seller; the other was to a member of her ninja gang. This kid and his snooping had to be stopped.

Chapter 12:
The Fugu

After finishing his snack, Jack hopped
back onto the Scatta-Scooter and made
his way over to Madame Midori's home. It
was in a quieter part of town.

Jack walked up to the front door and
knocked. Madame Midori opened the
door and grinned.

"Hello!" she said. She seemed very
excited to see Jack. "Why don't you come
in?"

Jack changed from his boots into the guest slippers, and followed Madame Midori through the building.

Jack looked around. It was a simple, yet pretty home. There were photos of Madame Midori everywhere. Most were of her singing into a microphone at her club.

"I am quite the karaoke entertainer," she said proudly. "I have won many singing competitions."

Jack pretended that he was impressed. They moved through the house and toward a grand room at the back. There was an ornate table in the middle and a large decorated chair against the back of the wall. Leading from the room was a sliding door that led to an outdoor garden.

"Please," Madame Midori said, "why don't you sit down?"

Jack knelt down on the mat and faced the table.

"I have asked my chef to prepare a special delicacy for you," she said, kneeling across from Jack. "It's a special Japanese fish called fugu."

Jack had never heard of fugu. He knew that in Japan a lot of interesting things were eaten, many of which he'd never tried before.

"Thank you," he said. "That's really nice of you to organize this for me. But I really just wanted to ask you some quick questions."

"We can do that in a little while," she said. "Here's some tea." She poured a cup of Japanese tea for Jack. He politely sipped a bit, although he didn't really like the taste of it.

"So anyway," Jack started. He wanted to hurry up the questioning. Jack didn't want to spend all day in Madame Midori's home.

"I wanted to show you this piece of paper," he said, opening the paper he'd taken from Mr. Taka's wall. "Do you recognize the handwriting?"

"No," she said, studying the paper. "I'm sorry." Not only was Madame Midori a good singer, she was also well-practiced in the skill of acting.

A man entered the room. He was dressed all in black and was carrying a tray with a single plate on it.

"Aha!" she said. "Here's the fugu. I'm a bit full right now, so I'll let you eat it all by yourself."

Jack was pretty full too. After all, he'd just had a tasty squid snack. But he didn't want to insult his host. He smiled and said "Itadaki-masu," which meant "thanks for the food."

Using chopsticks, he grabbed the fleshy meat. He bit into the fugu and then started to chew.

Madame Midori looked at him. A smirk grew across her face. "I hope you enjoy your food," she said. Her smirk turned into a sinister growl. "It will be the last thing you ever eat."

Chapter 13:
The Poison

As soon as Jack heard this, he quickly
spat out his food. What was she talking
about? And why was she saying such
nasty things? Madame Midori started to
cackle with laughter.

Thoughts started rushing through Jack's
head. He looked at the "chef" who had
brought him his food. He was dressed all
in black. Mrs. Taka had seen a black
shadow scurry across her garden. Another

three figures came into the room and stood behind Madame Midori. Jack counted four men in total. There were four thefts in Tokyo last night. One of the crooks had left a paper behind with the name of Madame Midori's club on it.

Did Madame Midori hire these men to do her dirty work? Could Madame Midori be behind the most daring theft in Japanese history?

"There's no use fighting it," she said. "The poison of the puffer fish, or fugu, will kill you. It will paralyze your muscles and soon you will stop breathing."

Jack had to react—and fast. He dashed from the room and threw his body through the paper door that led to the garden. Tumbling forward, Jack landed near a pond filled with koi, another kind of Japanese fish.

"Leave him be. We can clean up his body later." Madame Midori snarled at the ninjas.

With Madame Midori and her goons inside, Jack was left alone in the garden. Already his lips and tongue were tingling. His throat was starting to go numb, sweat was coming out of his skin.

Reaching for his Book Bag, Jack pulled out his Antidote Pack and ripped open the box. He grabbed the syringe and looked for the antidote vial that he needed.

Jack could tell from his symptoms that the fugu contained a poison that affected his nervous system. It was stopping all communication from his nerves to the other parts of his body.

He plunged the vial marked "Nervous" into the syringe, and then pulled down his trousers a bit. He knew the fastest way to get the antidote into his body was to stick a needle in the upper part of his bottom.

He pressed the tab on the top of the syringe and released the serum into his veins. Jack's muscles started to shake and spasm. His heart rate began to drop. These weren't the side effects of the antidote. These were the fatal symptoms of the fugu's poison. The antidote wasn't working quickly enough.

Jack could feel his body being paralyzed. His muscles stiffened and he collapsed, he found it more and more difficult to breathe.

He tried to send kind thoughts to his mum, his brother, his father and his friends. In the background, he could hear Madame Midori. She was telling her men to "hurry up and pack away the treasures."

If Jack had a last wish, he wanted to

use it to get better. Most of all, he wanted to catch Madame Midori and make her pay for what she had done. Jack drew some shallow breaths and closed his eyes. It was time to let fate take its course.

Chapter 14:
The Recovery

As Jack lay there, he paid attention to the length of each of his breaths. After a little while, they seemed to grow longer and deeper. With each long breath, Jack's body felt a bit better.

The tingling in his tongue and lips eventually disappeared and his muscles started to grow stronger. In fact, he was able to sit up. All totaled, Jack figured that about ten minutes had passed.

Thank goodness for the antidote, he thought. That serum had saved his life. Just then, he could hear Madame

Midori. She was still barking commands at her men. Jack had to stop them now, or else the priceless treasures may never be seen again.

Jack called Chief Ito, whose voice mail was on. Jack left him a message and told him what happened. He asked him to send reinforcements, and gave him the location of Madame Midori's house.

Jack crept through the garden and hid under one of the windows. Peeking inside the house, he could see the ninjas putting the samurai sword, painting, kimono and pearls into cardboard boxes.

If Jack had any doubts about who was responsible, seeing this proved that Madame Midori was the mastermind behind the thefts.

Just then, he heard the woman. "Go outside and check for that boy," she ordered. "We need to get rid of him before anyone notices."

Jack watched as two of the ninjas left the house, slid open the broken door and stepped into the garden. They looked to the area around the pond.

Since they knew that fugu poison paralyzed its victims, they were surprised to see no one on the ground. They went back into the house to report that fact to Madame Midori.

"He's not there," said one.

"What do you mean, he's not there?" Madame Midori screeched in a huff. She left the house and looked for herself. When she couldn't find Jack anywhere, she became angry.

"Well find him!" she said. "He can't have gone far!" Storming back into the house, she went about overseeing the remaining packing.

The two ninjas returned to the garden. They began to look over the pond area again. Seeing them gave Jack an idea. If he could quietly trap these two, he could sneak into the house and catch the others later.

He reached into his Book Bag and pulled out his Net Tosser. The GPF Net Tosser was one of those gadgets that was useful on nearly every mission. It was a disc with an internal net that sprayed over crooks and caught them inside.

Jack crept toward the men slowly. Just as he was about to activate the Net Tosser, Jack accidentally stepped on a twig.

SNAP!

It was a quiet sound that made a big impact.

Instantly, the men turned toward Jack. For a moment they were shocked—after all, how did Jack survive? Their shock gave way to anger, and they ran toward Jack.

Quickly, Jack flung the Net Tosser their way. The long arms of the gadget reached out for the men, swirled around them, and then trapped them inside. The ninjas struggled helplessly, but they were definitely out of action.

Chapter 15:
The Second Round

The commotion outside had alerted the others that something was going on. This wasn't over yet, and Jack knew it. There were still two other ninjas and Madame Midori to deal with.

The first to come out were the ninjas. When they saw their buddies trapped in the net, they leaped over the pond and headed straight for Jack.

Jack ran in the other direction, but he

tripped on a stone. His body flew forward and his stomach landed in the dirt. Scrambling, he tried to get up but one of the ninjas grabbed onto his foot.

"You're not going to get away from me!" he yelled. "I've got too much money at stake!"

"Take that!" said Jack, as he kicked the man in the nose.

"Oww!" wailed the ninja.

With ninja number one tending to his bloody nose, Jack got to his feet again and started to run. Ninja number two was still chasing Jack.

Jack headed for a stone lantern just ahead. Looking over his shoulder, he could see the thug chasing from behind. Jack grabbed onto the top of the lantern and swung his body around, kicking the man in the gut as he passed.

"Arrgh!" yelled the ninja, as he tumbled backward.

Jack let go of the lantern and landed on his feet. Now he was in the middle of the two men. One had a bloody nose and the other had a hurt stomach. Needless to say, they weren't happy. They raised their batons and scowled at Jack. The two crooks already under the Net Tosser were cheering their other ninja friends on.

In times like these, the GPF usually told their agents to do their best to use one of their gadgets. After all, two adult men against one boy were pretty tough odds. But Jack couldn't think of a gadget that would get them both, especially since they were at opposite ends of the path.

Jack was going to have to defend himself. Thankfully his judo instructor Mr. Baskin had taught him a thing or two. It was time to try out some new moves. . . .

Chapter 16:
The Moves

Ninja number one and his bloody nose made his move.

"I told you to get lost," he growled. "You're not going to get in the way of my money!"

He lifted his baton and lunged at Jack. As he ran for him, Jack grabbed onto the man's sleeves. He slid on his heels, and as he was about to land on his bottom, yanked the man over his shoulders.

The man came tumbling forward and onto his back. This was called the "side drop" in judo.

With his mate on the ground, the other ninja aimed for Jack, who quickly scrambled to his feet. But it wasn't fast enough. The man grabbed onto Jack's belt with his right hand, lifted him with his left, and then threw him onto the ground and onto his back.

"Uggh," Jack said to himself. That really hurt.

As Jack lay there, he tried to gather his thoughts. That first judo move he did had worked brilliantly. Ninja number one wasn't expecting that kind of maneuver from a kid.

But it was obvious that this second guy was skilled in judo too. Ninja number two had just pulled a "belt drop" on Jack. There was no way he was going to be able to keep this up forever.

Both men were now standing over him. Jack was going to have to think of a distraction to get out of their clutches.

As the men bent down to pick him up, Jack lifted his Watch Phone and turned its face toward the two men. The GPF had just added one more feature to this device, and Jack was going to use it to buy some more time.

He punched the FLASH button on his gadget and closed his eyes. Instantly, a blinding white light came out of his Watch Phone, temporarily blinding the two men.

"Oww!" they yelled, as they rubbed their eyes.

This gave Jack the chance he needed.

He sprinted toward the house, jumped over a shrub and made his way for a drain pipe.

Shimmying upward, Jack climbed it until he reached the edge of the roof. Then, he lifted himself up and over to the tiles.

From this vantage point, he could see everything. By now, Madame Midori had come out of the house and was standing on a patio below Jack.

The ninjas had regained their sight, and were now on the gutter pipe, making their way up to the roof.

Seeing them in these positions gave Jack a brilliant idea. It wasn't often you had a chance like this, thought Jack, to catch three crooks all at the same time. He smiled to himself and reached into his Book Bag. This was going to be fun.

Chapter 17:
The Traps

Jack focused on Madame Midori first. He took his Wax Statue dust out of his Book Bag.

He tore open the pack and sprinkled it over her head. As the green dust settled over her hair and body, she became very still. Noises were coming out of her mouth, but she couldn't move her lips.

Since Madame Midori was so fond of herself, Jack figured she wouldn't mind

being turned into a statue, like the kind you'd see in a wax museum. For the next hour or so, she'd be frozen and on show for everybody to see. That is, until the chemical wore off.

Now it was on to those ninjas. Ninja number one had reached the roof. He was running across, kicking tiles off the roof as he went. Jack grabbed one more thing from his Book Bag. This was called the Gluey Goo.

The Gluey Goo looked like an aerosol can of fake cheese. But inside was some of the stickiest glue you could find. In fact, it could hold the weight of a man, which is exactly what Jack was going to use it for.

He popped the lid, and waited for the ninjas to get close. When they did, he sprayed the glue all over the roof and onto their feet. Within seconds, the Gluey Goo hardened, and the men were stuck in their tracks.

Ninja number one was hopping mad. He tried to step out of his shoes and run away, but the skin on his bare feet got stuck too. He yelped in pain as he tried to get free. But there was no use, he wasn't going anywhere. Jack gave the air a one-two punch in triumph.

Chapter 18:
The Chief Again

In the distance, Jack could hear the sound of sirens. It was the Tokyo police. They were coming to save the day.

When the chief made his way to the garden, he looked around. There was a frozen woman standing on the back patio, two men sulking under a net and another two glued by their feet to the roof. Needless to say, he was pretty surprised.

"So," he said to Jack. "What exactly happened here?"

"Well," said Jack. "Madame Midori masterminded the theft of the treasures and hired these four ninja goons to do it."

The chief looked at the woman. Her eyes were moving around but her body was frozen still.

"Hmmm," he said to Jack. "Any chance of turning her back to normal? It'll be a bit difficult getting her to sit down in the back of the police car like that."

"Yeah," said Jack. He couldn't help but giggle. "She'll be all right. The effects of the dust only last an hour."

"What about those guys?" asked the chief. He was pointing to the ninjas stuck to the roof.

"Just spray some water on the glue and it will release the men," said Jack.

Chief Ito ordered his men to get the

hose. As they sprayed ninja number one and the other guy, the men slipped off the roof and fell onto the ground. After wrestling with the police officers, they were eventually scooped up and carried away.

He could hear ninja number one shouting at him in the distance.

"I'm going to get you. . . . " he said, his voice trailing off.

"And these?" said the police chief, nodding in the direction of the men being held by Jack's Net Tosser.

"No problem," said Jack. He tapped a few commands into his Watch Phone. The net retracted itself and the men were set free. Well, not exactly. Police officers swarmed over them, put cuffs on and then carried them away too.

"Well," said Chief Ito. "It looks like you've solved the crime. The country of Japan can't thank you enough."

"No worries," said Jack humbly. "It's my job. The treasures are in the house. They're stashed away in cardboard boxes."

Chief Ito thanked Jack again, and the two of them said their farewells. Jack walked across the garden and toward the house. As he passed Madame Midori he looked up at her. Her eyes were moving frantically back and forth. She was trying to say something to Jack.

"I know," said Jack. "You're trying to tell

me 'thank you.' It's my pleasure to have captured you and help send you to jail."

Jack gave her a wink and then walked off. He could hear Madame Midori screaming inside. That wasn't what she wanted to tell Jack. Jack had done his job and he was proud of himself. Yet another collection of criminals behind bars.

He smiled as he walked down the road and found a peaceful public garden, away from Madame Midori's house and the goings-on of the police department.

He reached into his Book Bag for his Portable Map. Whenever a secret agent was away on a mission there were many choices for getting home. You could find a real map and put a small flag on it. You could use an H button over the ground button on an elevator. If you were under-water in The Egg, you could program "home" as your destination. Or, you could use this—a small wooden foldout map that looked like your Magic Map at home.

Jack opened it on the ground and waited for the light inside England to glow. As it grew brighter, Jack yelled "Off to England!" Within moments, Jack was transported home.

Chapter 19:
The Starry Wish

When he arrived, Jack's bedroom was just as he left it. Whizzy was snoozing on Jack's bedside table and his Magic Map was still on the wall. On his desk was a copy of *The Samurai*, the book he'd been reading about before his latest adventure.

He packed it away in his school backpack, since he'd have to return it to the library tomorrow. Knowing it was time to get ready for bed, Jack brushed his teeth, yelled goodnight to his parents downstairs and got himself undressed for bed.

Crawling into bed, Jack turned out his side-table light. The room was dark, except for the glow-in-the-dark stars that were stuck to the ceiling above him. Jack remembered his Dad giving both him and Max a set of these stars when Jack was six and Max was eight. They took turns with their Dad sticking them in just the right place.

As Jack lay there remembering these happy times, he couldn't help but think about his brother. With Max gone, there was no one to talk to about his missions. And no one to yell "goodnight" to besides his Mum and Dad.

Closing his eyes, Jack wished on the stars above. He asked whoever was listening to give him another clue about his brother. With any luck, that critical piece of information was just around the corner. *Who knows,* thought Jack as he drifted off to sleep, *maybe that clue will come tomorrow.*

The Fight for the
Frozen Land:
ARCTIC
BOOK ⑫

The Fight for the Frozen Land:
ARCTIC

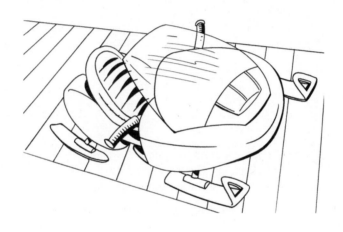

Elizabeth Singer Hunt

Illustrated by Brian Williamson

WEINSTEIN BOOKS

*For everyone working furiously to halt
climate change*

THE ARCTIC CIRCLE

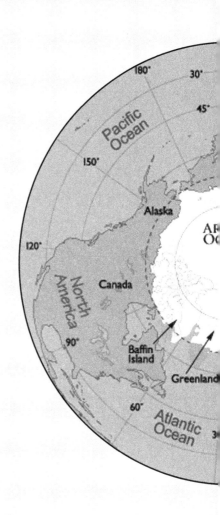

Destination:
ARCTIC

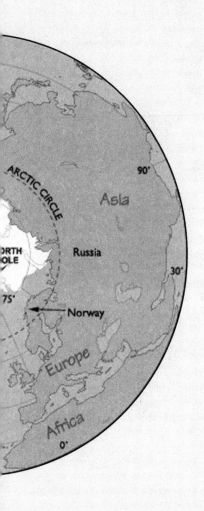

Jack Stalwart applied to be a secret
agent for the Global Protection
Force four months ago.

My name is Jack Stalwart. My older brother,

Max, was a secret agent for you, until he

disappeared on one of your missions. Now I

want to be a secret agent too. If you choose

me, I will be an excellent secret agent and get

rid of evil villains, just like my brother did.

Sincerely,

Jack Stalwart

THINGS YOU'LL FIND IN EVERY BOOK

Watch Phone: The only gadget Jack wears all the time, even when he's not on official business. His Watch Phone is the central gadget that makes most others work. There are lots of important features, most importantly the "C" button, which reveals the code of the day—necessary to unlock Jack's Secret Agent Book Bag. There are buttons on both sides, one of which ejects his life-saving Melting Ink Pen. Beyond these functions, it also works as a phone and, of course, gives Jack the time of day.

Global Protection Force (GPF): The GPF is the organization Jack works for. It's a worldwide force of young secret agents whose aim is to protect the world's people, places and possessions. No one knows exactly where its main offices are located (all correspondence and gadgets for repair are sent to a special P.O. Box, and training is held at various locations around the world), but Jack thinks it's somewhere cold, like the Arctic Circle.

Whizzy: Jack's magical miniature globe. Almost every night at precisely 7:30 P.M., the GPF uses Whizzy to send Jack the identity of the country that he must travel to. Whizzy can't talk, but he can cough up messages. Jack's parents don't know Whizzy is anything more than a normal globe.

The Magic Map: The magical map hanging on Jack's bedroom wall. Unlike most maps, the GPF's map is made of a mysterious wood. Once Jack inserts the country piece from Whizzy, the map swallows Jack whole and sends him away on his missions. When he returns, he arrives precisely one minute after he left.

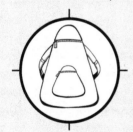

Secret Agent Book Bag: The Book Bag that Jack wears on every adventure. Licensed only to GPF secret agents, it contains top-secret gadgets necessary to foil bad guys and escape certain death. To activate the bag before each mission, Jack must punch in a secret code given to him by his Watch Phone. Once he's away, all he has to do is place his finger on the zip, which identifies him as the owner of the bag and immediately opens.

THE STALWART FAMILY

Jack's dad, John

He moved the family to England when Jack was two, in order to take a job with an aerospace company. Jack's dad thinks he is an ordinary boy and that his other son, Max, attends a school in Switzerland. Jack's dad is American and his mum is British, which makes Jack a bit of both.

Jack's mum, Corinne

One of the greatest mums as far as Jack is concerned. When she and her husband received a letter from a posh school in Switzerland inviting Max to attend, they were overjoyed. Since Max left six months ago, they have received numerous notes in Max's handwriting telling them he's OK. Little do they know it's all a lie and that it's the GPF sending those letters.

Jack's older brother, Max

Two years ago, at the age of nine, Max joined the GPF. Max used to tell Jack about his adventures and show him how to work his secret-agent gadgets. When the family received a letter inviting Max to attend a school in Europe, Jack figured it was to do with the GPF. Max told him he was right, but that he couldn't tell Jack anything about why he was going away.

Nine-year-old Jack Stalwart

Four months ago, Jack received an anonymous note saying: "Your brother is in danger. Only you can save him." As soon as he could, Jack applied to be a secret agent too. Since that time, he's battled some of the world's most dangerous villains, and hopes some day in his travels to find and rescue his brother, Max.

DESTINATION:
Arctic

The Arctic includes the northern parts of eight countries: Canada, Greenland, Russia, Alaska, Iceland, Norway, Sweden and Finland.

◻

Temperatures in the Arctic can range from around 45°F in the summer to minus 29°F in the winter.

◻

Polar bears, seals, walruses, beluga whales, narwhal whales, reindeer, arctic foxes and wolves live in the Arctic.

The word "Arctic" comes from the Greek word "Arktos," or "bear."

◻

The Arctic isn't actually a country, but an area of land, ice and water north of the Arctic Circle.

◻

GPF ANIMAL FACTS: THE POLAR BEAR

The polar bear is the world's largest land predator.

They are thought to have evolved from brown bears about 200,000 years ago, developing jagged teeth, large feet, a longer nose and short claws to hunt and survive in the extreme Arctic conditions.

Rising global temperatures is causing sea ice to melt. Although polar bears are excellent swimmers, they now have to travel further to find food.

Polar bears are listed as an "endangered species."

GPF FAST FACTS: GLOBAL WARMING

Global warming means that our planet's overall temperature is rising—by as much as 6.4 degrees in the next hundred years.

Greenhouse gases trap heat into our atmosphere, keeping us warm.
But levels of these gases, especially carbon dioxide, have recently risen to dangerous levels.

Many species will become extinct, and weather will become more extreme.

If we want to stop global warming from getting worse, we all have to work together as a team.

GPF GUIDE TO SAVING THE PLANET

Here's what you can do to help keep
our planet cool:

Turn the lights off when you
leave a room.

Use less water by turning the tap off
while you brush your teeth.

Encourage your family to bike and
walk places instead of using the car.

Recycle plastic and glass bottles,
aluminium cans, cardboard and paper.

Plant a tree somewhere—trees take
in carbon dioxide and give off
oxygen instead.

SECRET AGENT GADGET INSTRUCTION MANUAL

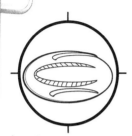

Sno-Sled: When you need to slide down a hill or pick up speed on a slick surface, use the GPF's Sno-Sled. Just pull out this oval-shaped plastic board, get a running start and sit on the middle. Make sure to hold onto the handles, as the Sno-Sled can travel at speeds of up to 80 mph.

Poison Tracker: When you need to analyze a mystery dust or liquid, use the GPF's Poison Tracker Kit. Use the gloves and the spoon to pick up the substance and place it into one of the glass vials. Within seconds the side of the vial will change color. Red means deadly; yellow is dangerous; and green is OK.

Sno-Speed: The GPF's Sno-Speed is the most technologically advanced and environmentally friendly snowmobile in the world. It travels over ice and snow at speeds of up to 200 mph, and uses a hydrogen fuel cell to make it go. It is equipped with a satellite navigation system, spotlights and a jagged knife on the side. Most impressive, it works by mind control. Just ask it to come, and it will find you.

Polar Parka: When you're working in freezing conditions, make sure you have your GPF Polar Parka. The Polar Parka is made of a special material that reacts to cold temperatures to keep your body comfortably warm. It has a glow-in-the-dark feature that enables others to find you if you're stranded or in trouble.

Chapter 1:
The Frozen Land

It was an early spring morning in the Arctic. Three scientists (two men and one woman) were standing over a table inside their warming hut. They were reviewing their map and preparing for the day's work. This was day number twenty-eight in their month-long assignment. Only a few more outings and they'd be ready to publish their findings.

"Let's take measurements from here

today," said the woman, pointing to a spot fifty miles away. "No one has collected data from this area before."

"Good idea," said another scientist. "It will be good to compare the thickness of the ice there with other locations."

The scientists pulled on their snowsuits and strapped on their boots. Stepping outside, they looked at the thermometer hanging by the door of the hut. The mercury read 20°F.

"Another warm day in one of the coldest places on Earth," said one. The other scientists chuckled at the joke.

After fastening their tools to their snowmobiles, they started the engines. Within moments, the trio was traveling across the frozen plain.

Within an hour, they'd arrived at their destination. They hopped off their snowmobiles and began organizing their tools. One of the scientists noticed some buildings in the distance. They looked like isolated warming huts.

"What are they?" said one.

"Let's check them out," said another.

As they walked toward the huts an enormous noise ripped through the air.

KABOOM!

Behind the buildings, chunks of ice and earth burst from the ground. The force of the explosion was so great, it knocked the trio off their feet.

Dazed, the scientists lay on their backs. Soon they were aware of another sound. This time it was the roaring sound of approaching snowmobiles, getting closer and closer.

BRRRM!

BRRRM!

"Who do you think that is?" said one of the men, looking scared.

"I don't know," said the woman.

The drivers of the snowmobiles had black helmets painted with flames and darkened visors covering their eyes.

"I have a bad feeling about this," said the other man.

"Me too," said the woman. "Let's get out of here."

The scientists crawled to their knees and began to run. They sprinted in the direction of their snowmobiles. If they

could get to a radio, they could call for help.

SWOOSH!

The first snowmobile slid in front, blocking their path. The scientists turned and ran the other way.

SWOOSH!

The second snowmobile trapped them from behind. Realizing what was happening, the trio looked around wildly.

"Don't hurt us," said one scientist. He put his hands in the air to show he didn't have any weapons.

"We won't tell anyone what we've seen," pleaded the woman. By now all of the scientists had their hands held high.

"We know you won't," sniggered one of the drivers. Pulling a long tube from his rucksack, he flashed it at the scientists.

"Please don't!" begged one of the men. Although he didn't know what the tube was for, he had a feeling it wouldn't be good news.

But the driver ignored their pleas. He aimed the tube at the scientists, and pumped the lever that was underneath. A fine dust burst into their faces. As it crept into their noses, they fell to the ground with a thud.

"Let's tie them up," said one driver to the other. "And kill their radios."

The drivers smashed the scientists' communication equipment. Then they tied them to the back of their snowmobiles. After congratulating each other on a job well done, the drivers left the area with the scientists' dazed bodies trailing behind.

Chapter 2:
The Warming Planet

Around the same time, but in a very different part of the world, Jack Stalwart was sitting at his desk, doing his homework. He'd been asked by his geography teacher, Mrs. Corry, to prepare a presentation on global warming. She wanted him to show that it existed, say what caused it and what, if anything, their class could do to help.

Jack knew that for many of his fellow

students the idea that the planet was warming up was a hard one to swallow. After all, England had just finished its coldest winter yet. Last spring there was snow on the ground at Easter! And last summer was one of the most pleasantly mild on record. But even though things at home seemed fine at the moment, global warming was causing wacky weather events elsewhere.

The southern states of America had just been battered by one of the worst hurricanes on record. In Europe, summer temperatures soared to 104°F (40°C) over a two week period. Last spring, a devastating cyclone hit Southeast Asia killing more than a hundred thousand people. And the scientific station in Antarctica recently reported that the Wilkins Ice Shelf—one of the continent's biggest—was about to crack and fall off into the sea due to melting.

Jack knew all of this thanks to the GPF. Jack was an agent for the Global Protection Force, or GPF; the only organization of young secret agents created to help protect the world. Rescuing an important person, a precious monument or priceless work of art were all examples of the kinds of things a GPF secret agent did.

For years the GPF had been working behind the scenes on global warming research. They were among the first to show that increases in carbon dioxide led to increases in global temperatures. In fact, the GPF had just sent out a team of scientists to research the effects of global warming on the Arctic. Jack had received a classified note about it via the secure GPF website.

Proving to his class that the planet was changing wasn't going to be difficult. He just needed to organize his facts and write them down. With that, he signed onto his computer, pulled up a blank document, and began to type out his report.

Chapter 3:
The White Card

Just then, Jack's Watch Phone began to
beep. It was almost 7:30P.M.—the time of
day when the GPF sent Jack the location
of his next mission.

After saving his document, Jack shut
the lid on his laptop. He walked over to
his bedside table and looked at Whizzy,
his miniature globe, who was just waking
up. Whizzy opened his eyes, winked at
Jack, and began spinning furiously in a

clockwise direction. Jack was definitely off on a mission tonight!

When Whizzy was ready, he coughed—"Ahem!"—and a jigsaw piece flew out of his mouth. It skimmed the top of Jack's duvet and glided like a model airplane across the room. When it landed smoothly on the floor, Jack rushed over to it. But when he got there, he was a bit confused.

Normally, when Whizzy spat something out, it was a jigsaw piece in the shape of a country. Jack would then take the piece to the Magic Map on his wall. When he matched it to the correct spot, the map would swallow him up and transport him to a new place.

But this piece wasn't in the shape of any country. In fact, it was just a small white rectangular card with a number code written on it. This could only mean one thing. The GPF's director, Gerald Barter, wanted to speak to Jack in person.

As he walked over to the map with the card, Jack's heart started to thump. He wondered why he was being summoned. Agents NEVER got to meet Gerald Barter in person unless they or someone else was in serious trouble.

The GPF had worked hard over the years to keep its true headquarter's location a secret, even from its own GPF agents. Agent training in gadgetry, martial arts and other areas had been held at top secret locations around the world. When an agent needed to repair a gadget, they had to send it via secure post to an anonymous P.O. Box. And when the GPF had to announce something to the press, it was always a one-way message with reporters unable to ask direct questions to the organization.

Jack had always figured it was somewhere cold and remote, but he didn't have any hard evidence. As he placed the rectangular card in a slot at the bottom right corner of the map, he took a deep breath. He was finally about to find out.

Chapter 4:
The Blinking Lights

As soon as Jack placed the card into a
space in the bottom right hand corner of
the map, lights began to appear all over—
first in Europe, then in Africa, then in
South America. Usually, a single light
appeared confirming the location of his
next adventure. But this time, the lights
were all over the place. The GPF wasn't
going to reveal the location of its
headquarters to Jack just yet.

Jack rushed over to his bed and grabbed his Book Bag from underneath. He checked his Watch Phone for the code of the day, keying it into his Book Bag's lock. The code word P-L-A-N-E-T didn't give Jack any clues either.

Looking inside, Jack checked his gadgets. There were the usual gadgets, like the Net Tosser, Noggin Mold and Poison Tracker. The presence of the Sno-Sled gave Jack a small hint of where it might be.

He rushed back to the Magic Map, strapping his Book Bag on tight. He waited as the lights on the map lit up at the same time. Not knowing exactly what country to say, Jack just yelled, "Off to the GPF!"

With that command and with a force he'd never experienced before, the lights burst and swallowed Jack into the Magic Map.

Chapter 5:
The Headquarters

When he arrived, Jack found himself
standing all alone in a bitingly cold and
quiet place. There was a steel door with a
screen in the middle facing him, and
another steel door behind. The ceiling
above and walls around him were made
of jagged rock. If Jack had to guess, he
was probably standing in the entranceway
to a building carved into a mountain.

He walked over to the screen on the

steel door. The sign above said: GPF Identification Lock. He leaned toward the screen and looked into it. A laser beam took a picture of his retina. The word IDENTIFIED flashed across the screen in green.

Then, an outline of a hand appeared on the screen. Jack placed his right hand over the drawing. His fingers lit up one by one and when the screen had read and recognized all five of his fingerprints, the door to the building unlocked.

Pushing it open, Jack walked through to the other side. Almost as soon as he did, his environment changed. He was standing

in a brightly lit room. People were rushing around carrying papers, while others were chatting away on their phones. Television screens scattered about were showing news about world events.

In front of him was a reception desk. The woman sitting there recognized Jack and smiled.

"Welcome Secret Agent Courage," she

said. "It's so nice to finally meet you in person."

Jack stood, taking it all in. He was at the headquarters of one of the most powerful crime-fighting forces around the world. Even though he was a part of it, he was still temporarily shocked.

"Hi," said Jack, clearing his throat. "I think you're expecting me."

"Yes, we are," she said. "I'll let Director Barter know that you're here." She tapped on an earpiece she was wearing and spoke into a microphone hidden in the cuff of her sleeve.

"Secret Agent Courage is here to see you," she said.

After listening to the reply, she looked up at Jack. "Director Barter will see you now," she said. "Just take the elevator to the second floor. His office will be straight in front of you."

Jack looked past the receptionist. There were two tubelike lifts made of glass that carried passengers to various levels. From Jack's count, there looked to be at least four levels to the GPF HQ.

As Jack made his way to the elevators, he walked by the most amazing looking snowmobile he'd ever seen. It was sitting in the middle of the floor with a sign posted next to it.

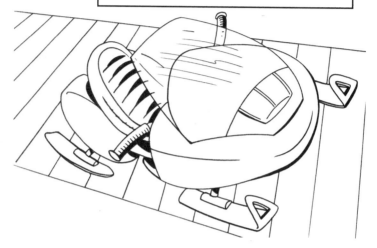

GPF SNO-SPEED.
MOST POWERFUL SNOWMOBILE IN THE
WORLD. CAPABLE OF DRIVING ON ICE AND
SNOW AT SPEED OF 200 MPH.
HYDROGEN POWERED. YET ANOTHER GPF
GADGET COMING SOON.

"WOW," thought Jack. "Max would have loved to have seen this." He and his brother, who had gone missing in action while on a GPF assignment, loved fast things.

Tapping the number 2 button on the wall, Jack called for the elevator. When it arrived, the doors opened. A man came out, brushing past Jack.

"Hey," he said, spinning around. "You're Secret Agent Courage!" The man put his hand out to Jack. "Thanks for taking care of that mess with the poachers in Kenya," he said.

Jack was a bit embarrassed. This must be what it felt like to be famous!

"Don't mention it," he said sheepishly, putting his hand out to the man. The man excitedly shook it and then let it go.

"Keep up the good work!" he said, as he patted Jack on the back and walked away.

Jack stepped into the elevator, pushing the right button. It climbed until it reached the second floor.

PING!

The doors opened wide. In front of him was another door. A sign read:

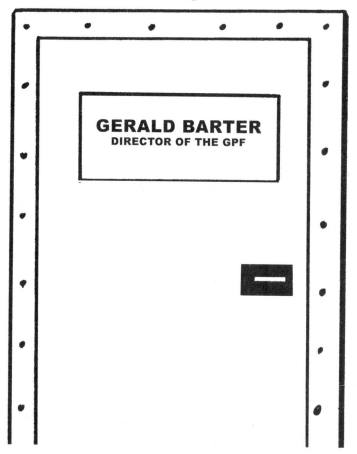

GERALD BARTER
DIRECTOR OF THE GPF

Chapter 6:
The Man in Charge

Jack walked up to the door and tried to re-lax. He took a deep breath and straightened his clothes. But his stomach was doing flips and his heart was beating fast.

Stop it, he told himself. There's nothing to be nervous about. Think about Director Barter as an ordinary guy. He uses the toilet like everybody else, chews his food like everybody else and probably snores as loud as Dad.

But imagining Gerald Barter as an ordinary person wasn't working for Jack. After all, Mr. Barter was the head of one of the most influential agencies in the world. Most important, he was one of the few people who probably knew something about his brother Max.

Swiftly Jack's thoughts went to his brother. Then a horrible idea struck him. Maybe the director had called him to tell him some terrible news.

Jack gulped and knocked twice.

"Come in," said a voice from the other side.

Turning the handle, Jack pushed the door open. Sitting at a desk at the back of the room was none other than Gerald Barter himself.

"Come in," he said to Jack again. "Close the door behind you."

Jack did as he was told. As he made his way over to the director, he found himself walking on toughened glass. Under the clear flooring was a flattened map of the world. It would have been identical to the Magic Map in Jack's room, if it weren't for the twinkling red lights all over.

"We call that our 'hot zone' map," said the director. "The red lights show us areas of criminal activity." As Jack studied the map, he noticed a few more red lights come up.

"I'm afraid crime never goes away," said the director. "Anyway," he added, pointing to the chair in front of his desk, "why don't you sit so we can talk."

Jack made himself comfortable. The GPF regularly sent pictures of the director out to the press, but they looked nothing like the man seated across from him. This man was handsome, with dark skin and no glasses. The pictures Jack had seen were of a man with lighter skin and thick-rimmed glasses.

Clever, thought Jack. The GPF had been giving the world fake pictures of the director. That way, he'd never be recognized in a crowd, or be the target of a notorious crook.

"The reason I have called you is because we have a serious problem," Barter said.

Jack closed his eyes and hoped there was no bad news about Max.

"Three of our scientists have vanished from here in the Arctic," Barter said. "We need you to locate them and bring them back to safety."

Phew, thought Jack as he opened his eyes. While he wasn't pleased to hear about the scientists, he was relieved there wasn't a terrible development about his brother. Interestingly, the director had said "here in the Arctic," which meant GPF HQ must be somewhere near the North Pole. It would explain why he was so cold when he first arrived.

"Were these the scientists studying global warming?" asked Jack.

The director nodded in agreement. He seemed pleased that Jack was on top of the latest GPF news.

"Here they are," said Barter, showing

Jack a collection of photos taken of the team. "Study their faces so you can recognize them later. They checked in yesterday morning before they set off," he explained. "They didn't tell us where they were going; only that it was unchartered territory. Unfortunately, we haven't heard from them since."

"Maybe they're still at work," said Jack. "Perhaps they decided to camp out and return later than expected."

"That's not possible," said Barter. "They're under strict instructions to report back to the hut. After all, nighttime temperatures are extremely low and there are hungry polar bears roaming about."

"I'm assuming they would have traveled by snowmobile," said Jack. "What about their radios?" All GPF snowmobiles were equipped with sophisticated communication and navigation equipment.

"We're getting nothing but static," said Barter. "Someone or something has disabled their systems."

The whole thing did seem strange to Jack. How could a team of scientists completely vanish? There was no way a single polar bear could have brought down three adults. Maybe, thought Jack, they'd fallen through the ice.

"Can you show me where their warming

hut was located?" asked Jack. He figured it would be a good place to start looking for clues.

"Here," said the director, pointing to a map on his desk. His finger was showing an area 150 miles away.

"Then that's where I'll begin," said Jack. Before he got up, Jack thought of another question. "If you don't mind me asking, why didn't you send somebody else—somebody based here at the GPF HQ?"

"Because," said the director with a smile, "I needed my best agent for this job. I don't need to tell you how critical this mission is. The work of these scientists could have a major impact on our lives here on Earth."

Jack agreed. Aside from finding his brother, he couldn't think of a bigger mission. He wanted to ask Director Barter something about Max. As he opened his mouth, the director chimed in.

"Look," he said, almost reading Jack's mind. "I know this thing with your brother has been difficult. We're doing our best to try and locate him. As soon as we do," he added, "we'll let you know."

Jack acted relieved, but something was still nagging at him. The tone of the director's voice and his body language hinted that he knew something more. But Jack couldn't very well challenge him without any solid evidence. Not here. Not now.

"I'll do my best to find the scientists," said Jack, focusing on the mission at hand.

"Thank you," said the director. "Why don't you take the elevator to the ground level. Mr. Davidson has something for you."

Mr. Davidson was the GPF's technology wizard. He'd single-handedly designed and built nearly every gadget in the GPF arsenal. He'd been working for the GPF ever since it began. The Hypno-Disc, the Torpedo, the Flyboard and the Melting Ink Pen were just some of his fantastic creations.

Jack took the map from the director's desk and rushed to the door. He was excited—it wasn't every day an agent got to meet the man responsible for some of the greatest GPF gadgets of all time.

Waving goodbye to the director, Jack stepped back into the hallway. He took the lift to the ground level. When he got there, he found himself staring at another steel door. On it was another sign that said: SPEAK. Jack said "hello," and when the door recognized his voice, it slid open.

Chapter 7:
The Tech Guy

"Welcome, Secret Agent Courage!" boomed
a voice.

It was Mr. Davidson, and he was
standing in the middle of an underground
warehouse. Jack guessed the lanky man
was sixty years old, but given how
animated he was he could have been
decades younger.

"It's so nice to meet you," he said,
quickly approaching. He grabbed Jack's

hand and shook it furiously. After he was
finished, Jack put his throbbing hand in
his pocket.

"This is where it all happens!" Mr.
Davidson said, spinning around on his
heels. He was showing Jack one of the
biggest collections of super spy gadgets
in the world.

Mr. Davidson led Jack around the room
by the elbow. They passed by hundreds
of high-tech gadgets, many that Jack
recognized and many more that he
didn't.

"Why don't we come over here," said
Mr. Davidson, leading Jack to a stepladder
in the middle of the room. "I want to
show you something," he added.

They climbed the steps together until

the ladder stopped at the edge of a platform. On the platform was something large underneath a beige tarpaulin.

"When Director Barter told me what you were up to, I decided to put a rush on this." With one stroke of the hand Mr. Davidson pulled off the tarpaulin, unveiling the hidden object.

Jack stared at none other than the GPF Sno-Speed—the high-tech snowmobile he'd seen in the reception area.

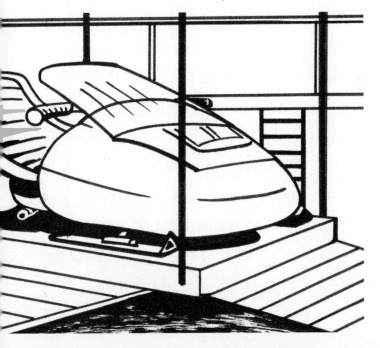

"You're joking," said Jack, who couldn't believe his luck. "You mean I get to ride this thing? Wow!"

"Yep!" said Mr. Davidson. "Consider yourself the 'test' agent."

Mr. Davidson showed Jack around the vehicle and how to activate its hydrogen-powered engine. He then demonstrated how several of its features worked. At the front was a satellite navigation screen, as well as a spotlight for seeing things in the dark. Tucked away into a door on the side was a sharp, serrated knife. On the dash was a "silencer" button that would turn the noise of the engine completely off.

Lastly, and most impressive, Mr. Davidson told Jack how the "mental telepathy" feature worked. If Jack was lost or in trouble, all he had to do was call the vehicle with his mind. The Sno-Speed would start up and find him wherever he was.

"Impressive," Jack said to Mr. Davidson, although he secretly doubted something like that would actually work.

"And I have something else for you," Mr. Davidson said, dashing down the ladder and to a closet at the back of the warehouse. When he returned, he was carrying a thin yellow parka.

"Wear this," he said. "It will help keep you warm. Those Arctic winds are freezing."

Jack had read about the GPF's Polar Parka. It was made of a special fabric that reacted to outside temperature. The colder it got outside, the warmer it got on the inside. What was also great about the Polar Parka was that it glowed in the dark. So if an agent was lost in a snowstorm or at night, they would be easier to find.

"Thanks," said Jack, slipping on the Polar Parka under his Book Bag and climbing onto the Sno-Speed.

"How do I look?" Jack asked.

"Super!" replied Mr. Davidson. "But you need a helmet."

"Right," said Jack, who pulled his Noggin Mold out of his Book Bag.

Once the flexible plastic had hardened to Jack's head, Mr. Davidson rushed down the steps and over to a big green button on the opposite wall. He punched it, opening another sliding door. A cold blast of wind and snow flurries flew in.

"Now be careful," he warned. "I don't want to be reading about you getting into trouble in the next edition of the GPF News!"

"Don't worry," said Jack. "I'll try and make sure that doesn't happen."

He started the engine and positioned

the nose of the snowmobile over the ramp below. With a twist of the accelerator, the Sno-Speed flew through the warehouse and out into the snow.

Chapter 8:
The Hut

Almost as soon as Jack was outside in the daylight, he turned around to wave to Mr. Davidson. But there was nothing behind him but a mountain covered in snow. There was no sign of the door he'd come through, nor any hint of the GPF headquarters inside. He wondered whether he'd dreamed the whole thing, but after looking at his Polar Parka and Sno-Speed he knew what had happened was real.

Jack pulled out the map that Gerald Barter had given him. He looked to the coordinates of the warming hut. Programming them into the navigation screen on the Sno-Speed, Jack put his paper map away. He sat for a moment and looked around. The Arctic was absolutely stunning. It was the most beautiful place Jack had ever seen.

It was early spring, which meant after months of being barely above the horizon, the sun was back in the sky. Now that it was shining, the ground was a glittering white and the sky a crystal blue. The ice and snow went on for miles.

After traveling for a while, he saw a small building up ahead. According to his navigation device, this was the scientists' warming hut. Jack pulled up alongside the weatherproof building, and began to look for clues.

But there was nothing to be found. There was a thermometer, a few solar

panels on the roof, an outhouse and an empty tool box. There weren't any tracks from the team's snowmobiles or signs of a struggle with a polar bear. Whatever had happened to them must have happened after they left. But where did they go? Because it looked like it had recently snowed, Jack couldn't tell which direction they had gone.

Maybe, Jack reckoned, searching inside would give him an idea. Using his Magic Key Maker, Jack unlocked the door and stepped inside.

The hut was one large room. In front of him were three beds, and to his right was a small kitchen. To his left was a lounge area with a simple communication system. In the center of the room was an aluminum table. The table had a sheet of paper on top. Jack walked over and studied it carefully.

But this wasn't just any piece of paper. It was a map. Colored lines were drawn from an *X* in the middle outward. Jack figured the *X* was the location of the warming hut. The lines marked the routes the scientists had traveled. At the end of each line was a dot, and next to each dot was a handwritten date.

If Jack could find a dot with yesterday's

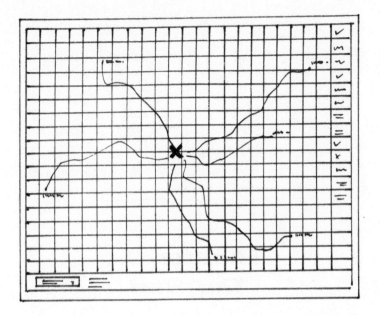

date, he could trace the path the scientists had taken. Spying a blue dot with the right date, Jack made a note of the coordinates. He rushed out of the hut, jumped on his Sno-Speed and programmed the details of his next destination.

"Don't worry," said Jack out loud. "I'm coming to rescue you." And then he sped off.

Chapter 9:
The Find

Jack and his Sno-Speed traveled at a
blistering pace over the Arctic ice. The
screen on the Sno-Speed not only told
him how fast he was going (90 mph) but
also whether there was ice or land or a
combination of both below. As he
traveled, the ice-covered land changed to
ice alone. Jack was now speeding along
on top of the frozen Arctic Sea.

In the distance, he could see a polar

bear—one of the most feared killers of the Arctic. Male polar bears could weigh up to around 1,540 pounds and grow as long as a one-story building. They mostly preyed on seals, but Jack knew if they were desperate they'd pretty much eat anything. As he sat on his Sno-Speed, Jack was relieved that he was far away. The last thing he wanted was to be within striking distance of a creature like that.

Further ahead, he could see something in the glistening snow. It looked like a trio of snowmobiles. Jack increased his speed and hurried along.

When he got there, he recognized them as the wrecked snowmobiles of the missing scientists. No wonder Director Barter wasn't able to get a signal, thought Jack. Their communication systems were pretty bashed up. But where was the team?

Jack walked around the vehicles looking for clues. In front of them, he spied some footprints. Following them as they traveled north, he noticed they doubled back on themselves. Somewhere in the mess of footprints, Jack noticed something pink glistening in the snow. He knelt down to get a better look. It resembled a fine pink dust.

Not sure what it was or whether to

touch it, Jack pulled out his Poison Tracker device. The GPF's Poison Tracker was an all-in-one kit that could analyze any substance (liquid or dry) and tell an agent whether to beware. If the glass on the vial turned red it meant the substance was deadly. Yellow meant dangerous. Green meant it was harmless.

Slipping on his protective gloves, Jack scooped up the dust with a small spoon and tapped it into a glass vial. He put the top on and shook it hard. Within seconds, the vial turned yellow. DANGEROUS.

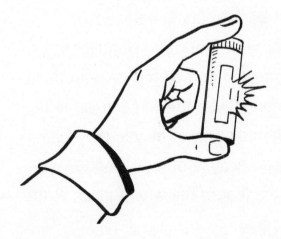

Jack snapped off his gloves and put them away. The scientists seemed to have been drugged, but with what? Maybe it was a paralyzing potion that had crippled their muscles. Or, maybe it was a dozing dust. Either way, Jack had to figure out where they were—and fast.

He looked to the ground again. Traveling from where he stood were snowmobile tracks different than those made by GPF vehicles. He followed the marks with his eyes, and saw that they led to some huts in the distance. Jack hurried back to his Sno-Speed.

If Jack was right, the scientists had been drugged and carted away to those buildings. Maybe they'd seen something they shouldn't have. Maybe they were captured because of their work. Maybe they were just in the wrong place at the wrong time.

But those possible reasons didn't really matter. What mattered to Jack was that innocent people were being held hostage. Those poor scientists were probably dazed, cold and hungry.

It was these thoughts that filled Jack's mind. With the faces of the scientists burned on his brain, Jack pushed the silencer button on the Sno-Speed's engine and set off. The wind against Jack's face felt even colder now. In the beautiful but harsh Arctic, there was never a moment to waste.

Chapter 10:
The Tipped Cane

As Jack approached the buildings, he counted three huts. The one in front was large, while the other two were much smaller. Surrounding the back was a fence made of barrels. Jack navigated the Sno-Speed toward it and stopped the engine.

Climbing off the vehicle, he crouched down and scurried along the fence. Out of nowhere, Jack heard two men talking. He dropped to the ice and held his breath.

"What should we do?" said one voice.

"Let's lay some more tarp," said the
other.

Jack risked a peek over the barrels. The
two men were wearing black helmets with
flames on the sides. Although their visors
were lifted, Jack couldn't see much of
their faces.

Heading to one of the smaller huts, the men flung open the doors. Jack could see large rolls of black tarpaulin stacked high inside. The men clambered to the top of the pile and rolled two down. They then lugged them through the snow and attached them to their snowmobiles.

"Will those geeks be OK without us?" asked one, climbing onto his vehicle.

"Yeah," said the other, doing the same. "They're not going anywhere."

They started their snowmobiles and took off. Jack wasn't sure what they were doing with that tarp, but he knew one thing—these were the guys who had snatched the scientists. And because of what they'd said, he knew the team was inside one of the huts.

Running along the fence, Jack headed to the main building. The front door was locked, so he used his Magic Key Maker.

After pushing this thin piece of plastic into the keyhole, it melted and then hardened to form a perfect key. Jack turned the lock and the door popped open. As soon as he was inside, he began looking around. The rooms were separated by hanging sheets of weather-proof material. It was like a mega-sized family tent, the kind Jack's family took on camping holidays to the New Forest.

Dashing from one room to the next,

Jack pushed the sheets as he went. In one of the rooms, he saw an open laptop. On the screen was a draft of an e-mail waiting to be sent. Jack read it carefully. It was addressed to an ag@woandg.com.

Project Black Arctic is proceeding well. Only a few more weeks and Phase I will be complete.
Regards,
G. R. Slick

Except for the GPF's global warming research, Jack wasn't aware of any other legal projects going on in the Arctic. He wondered what the phrase "Black Arctic" meant, and which of the two men was G. R. Slick.

He was about to re-read the e-mail when a male voice shouted at him from behind. "What are you doing in my office?"

Startled, Jack turned around to see someone altogether different from the two men he'd seen before. This man was tall with greasy black hair, and a face that hadn't been shaved in days. His two front teeth stuck out like a beaver's, and his feet were the length of two small boats. Since the man referred to the area as his office, Jack figured he was G. R. Slick.

"Answer me!" he shouted at Jack. "What the devil are you doing reading my personal e-mails?"

From behind, the man pulled out a wooden cane. He whacked Jack's body with it as hard as he could.

"Arrgh!" Jack yelled in agony, and collapsed to the floor.

As the pain wore off, Jack stood up to face Mr. Slick. When he did, Mr. Slick put the tip of the cane between his eyes. At its tip was a sharp metal point. Jack knew if he moved, Mr. Slick could blind him with one poke.

"Now," said Mr. Slick, "I'll ask you one more time." He leaned in further. "What are you doing snooping around?"

Just then, Jack heard footsteps. The two men he'd seen outside had come back.

"What's the matter, boss?" they asked.

They were breathing heavily, as if they'd been running.

Jack thought carefully about what to do next. He decided the best thing to do was to trick Mr. Slick into keeping him alive.

"My name is Jack Jones," he said. "And I work for the Worldwide Animal Group. We're researching polar bears in the Arctic. You know," he added quickly, "tracking their moves and documenting how they take care of their young."

Mr. Slick and his men were glaring at him but listening. Jack carried on.

"I saw these huts," he explained, "and I thought perhaps you were part of my group. The Worldwide Animal Group said they were sending other researchers out here. So I came in to have a look."

Jack waited for a response. Mr. Slick started to laugh, soon joined by the other two men. But this wasn't a funny ha-ha kind of laugh. It was much more sinister than that.

"You expect me to believe that?" cackled Mr. Slick. "You know what I think," he said, turning to his men. "I think this punk has come looking for his friends. Why don't we put him with the others?"

With Mr. Slick's cane still pointed between Jack's eyes, one of his men lifted a long tube and pumped a lever underneath. Mr. Slick backed away. The other two men put their visors down.

Within moments, a fine pink dust was released into the air around Jack's nose. He frantically tried to cover his nostrils, but it was too late. The dangerous dust had entered his body.

"You're going to regret messing with me," said Mr. Slick.

The next thing Jack knew, his body felt heavy. Within seconds everything went black.

"Pick him up," snarled Mr. Slick, as he pointed to Jack's limp body. "And keep your eyes out for more trespassers," he growled. "It seems as though everybody and their grandmother is in the Arctic today."

With that, Mr. Slick twirled on the point of his cane. He left the hut and his men to do what they were ordered. They scraped Jack's body off the floor and carried him away.

Chapter 11:
The Reason

Jack wasn't sure how long he'd been drugged, but when he finally came to it felt like an eternity. His body was stiff and achey and he could barely open his eyes. In the background, he could hear voices.

"Is that who I think it is?" said one.

"I think so," said another.

"Do you think he's come here to help?" asked a third.

Jack found himself lying sideways on

the floor. Staring at him from across the way were three people: one woman and two men. Jack recognized their faces from the pictures in Director Barter's office. They were the missing scientists. Now all he had to do was get himself off of the floor, call the GPF and get rid of those nasty men for good.

But Jack couldn't move. His wrists and feet were tied together. There was no way he could reach his Watch Phone.

"It won't work," said one of the scientists. "They're pretty good at tying people up." With their eyes, they motioned to Jack to show that they too had been tied up.

"My name is Elsa," said the woman scientist.

"I'm Ted," said one of the men.

"And I'm Jordan," said the last.

Jack began to introduce himself too, but Elsa interrupted. "We know who you are," she said.

Again, Jack was a bit embarrassed. This was the second time in a short while that someone had recognized him for his secret agent skills and success rate.

"So," said Jack. "Tell me what happened."

Ted started first. "We came out this way," he said, "to measure the thickness of the ice. As we were getting our gear together, Jordan noticed these huts."

"So we decided to check them out," added Jordan, "and these goons came out of nowhere. They sprayed us with dust, and that's how we ended up here."

"Did you see anyone or anything else?" asked Jack.

"There was a big explosion," said Elsa.

"What kind of explosion?" asked Jack.

"The kind you get with dynamite," said Ted. "It blew up large chunks of the ice."

Jack thought about Mr. Slick's e-mail.

He wondered if blowing up bits of Arctic ice was part of this "Black Arctic" project. He wondered what else was part of his plan.

"In one of the smaller huts," said Jack, "I saw loads of rolled-up black tarp. Any idea what that could be about?"

They all thought for a moment, and then Elsa, the female scientist, gasped.

"What's the matter?" asked Jack.

"Well," she said. "It's only an idea. But it makes sense."

Jack and the men listened as she spoke.

"The Arctic," Elsa said, "is heating up more than any place on Earth. There's less white ice available to reflect the sun's energy back. Since there is less ice and more dark water, the exposed water is making the melting worse."

The men nodded in agreement and all three looked at Jack.

"According to our work here this spring," she added, "Ted, Jordan and I are estimating that the Arctic may lose all of its ice by 2030. That is, unless we try to stop global warming. If I'm right," she added, "these men are trying to hurry it up."

"By breaking up the ice and using the black tarp to absorb more heat?" asked Jack.

Elsa nodded.

"But why would they want to do that?" yelled Jordan in frustration. "They must be nuts! Our planet is already in crisis. Don't they know it would make matters worse?"

"Maybe they do, and maybe they don't," said Jack. "The important thing is that we have to stop them."

Jack wondered why they were doing all

of this, and then he remembered the e-mail he'd seen. Mr. Slick had written to an ag@woandg.com. If Jack could figure out who that was, it might help him answer the "why."

Chapter 12:
The Evil Plan

Just then, the door banged open.

BLAM!

A cold rush of air swept in. It was
Mr. Slick and his men. Jack looked
desperately at his Watch Phone. If only he
could reach the key pad with the fingers
on his right hand.

Mr. Slick noticed Jack glancing at his
wrist. "What have we here?" he said,
leaning down to Jack's level. "Is that one

of those silly radio devices?"
Mr. Slick's bony fingers
pried the gadget off
Jack's wrist. Standing
up with it in his
hand, he tilted it
and then
looked at its
underside.

"Yes," he said to his men. "I think we should definitely get rid of this."

Then he threw the gadget to the ground, lifted his cane and with one thrust of its metal spike split it in two.

"There," he said, kicking the pieces across the floor. "That should stop you from calling for help."

As Jack sat in momentary shock, he realized Mr. Slick wasn't finished yet. His evil eyes were fixed on Jack.

"I've heard there's some polar bear activity in this area," he carried on. "And since you were part of the—what did you call it—Worldwide Animal Group," he said, "I thought you'd like to see one up close. Lucky you!"

Jack narrowed his eyes back to Mr. Slick. He didn't like the sound of him or his plan. But at this point, Jack didn't have any choice but to go along. He'd have to look for another opportunity to escape.

"Drag them out!" ordered Mr. Slick.

Mr. Slick's henchmen pulled Elsa, Ted and Jordan from their seats and out of the door. Although they shouted for help as best as they could, their cries were swallowed up by the icy wilderness.

Then the men came back for Jack. They grabbed him by the arms and dragged him outside. There was a trailer attached to one of the snowmobiles. Forcing all four of them onto it, the bad guys climbed on top of their snowmobiles.

As they traveled south, Jack wondered what Mr. Slick was planning. Was he going to leave them out there alone? Or was he planning something else?

Hoping it was the former, Jack thought through his options.
Not too far away, he saw a large polar bear on the horizon. Mr. Slick looked at Jack, baring his horrible yellow teeth.

"I'm going to get you!" Jack snarled at Mr. Slick.

Laughing, Mr. Slick ordered his goons to keep moving ahead. When they were within 100 yards of the bear, the men slowed down. Mr. Slick spoke to Jack and the scientists.

"This is as far as we're going," he said. "I personally don't want to be within a whiff of that bear. We'll be leaving you here to fend for yourselves. I'm sure it will come and say hello in no time!"

Mr. Slick's men lugged the scientists and Jack out of the trailer. They tossed the four of them onto the snow.

"Toodles," said Mr. Slick. "Happy eating!"

Then Mr. Slick and his men left them alone on the ice.

Chapter 13:
The Savior

"We have to get out of here!" cried Elsa. "That bear's going to smell us!"

Almost as soon as she said that, Jack saw the bear lift its nose in the air. It had done what Mr. Slick predicted, it had gotten a whiff of their scent and was making its way over.

"Hurry!" yelled Ted. Everyone was yanking at their ties, trying to wriggle free.

"Don't worry," said Jack. "I have a plan."

He closed his eyes and concentrated hard. Jack was trying to call his Sno-Speed.

When Mr. Davidson showed Jack around the Sno-Speed, he had told him about its "mental telepathy" feature— the ability to read an agent's mind. All Jack had to do was think very hard and the Sno-Speed would come to get him. Thanks to the transponder Jack wore on his body, it would also know where to go.

"It's coming!" shouted Jordan.

Jack opened his eyes. Unfortunately, Jordan wasn't talking about the Sno-Speed. He was talking about the bear. The noise and their scent had drawn it to them. It was now running toward them— at a frightening rate.

Desperately the foursome rolled to their sides and got to their feet. They were hopping as best as they could in an attempt to get away.

But Jack and the scientists knew it was no use. Polar bears could run at 25 miles per hour. Given its current speed and the short distance between them, Jack figured it would arrive within seconds.

Just then, Jack saw a yellow blur out of the corner of his eye. He looked to his right. There was the Sno-Speed! Mr. Davidson had come up trumps again with another life-saving gadget.

On seeing the Sno-Speed, the bear stopped in its tracks. Confused and wondering what this strange object was, the bear turned and loped off in the other direction.

The Sno-Speed glided in front of Jack. Jack bent down and twisted himself, so that his wrists were up against its side. He pushed a button that released a small, jagged knife from the side compartment. Grabbing onto it with his fingers, he sawed through the rope on his wrists. He then cut himself free at the feet. One by one he released the scientists too.

"So," said Jordan, "what's next?" Jack climbed on top of the Sno-Speed and turned on the main screen. He sent an e-mail to Director Barter telling him what had happened, and calling for reinforcements. Unfortunately, Jack knew that it would still take them a while to get there.

Just then, another explosion could be heard. Jack and the scientists saw huge chunks of ice fly into the air and back onto the ground.

"Those guys have to be stopped—and now," said Jack. "Unfortunately, I have to do this myself."

The scientists knew that GPF agents worked alone, or with other people so long as they wouldn't get in the way. There were three adults in addition to Jack. There was no way he could take all of them along.

Reaching into his Book Bag, Jack pulled out a small disc made out of nylon. This was the GPF's Base Camp. When Jack threw it to the ground, it fanned open into a large weatherproof tent. He rummaged around his Book Bag and pulled out the GPF's Portable Tea Makers. They may not be strictly life-saving gadgets, but these collapsible cups containing tea bags would be a comfort to the scientists stuck in the cold. The last thing he gave them was a bottle of water.

"Just pour that into those cups and

you'll be fine," said Jack, climbing back
onto his Sno-Speed. Jack knew the cups
contained a thermostat that would heat
the water themselves. "Thanks, Jack,"
said Elsa. "We know you can do it."

"You're the best," said Ted, giving Jack
a high-five.

"No worries," said Jack. "I'll stop these guys."

He waved goodbye to the scientists, just as another bomb went off in the distance.

KABOOM!

Chapter 14:
The Hole in the Ice

Finding Mr. Slick and his henchmen would be easy, thought Jack. He'd just have to follow the exploding ice. As he traveled, Jack spied large sheets of black tarp covering the ground. Not too far away were Mr. Slick and one of his men. They were busy looking at something on the ground. Their backs were to Jack, so it was a perfect time to strike.

With the silencer still on the Sno-Speed,

Jack aimed it straight for them. He stood up to give himself leverage and pulled his Net Tosser out of his Book Bag. Just as he was about to throw it over the crooks, something hit him from behind.

SMACK!

Jack's body was hurled over the handlebars and onto the snow. As he lay there stunned, he saw another snowmobile drive by. On it was the second of Mr. Slick's men. He laughed as he skidded past Jack.

Quickly Jack started to run. He still had the Net Tosser in his hands. Sprinting as fast as he could, he flung the gadget in Mr. Slick's direction. But Mr. Slick hobbled out of the way. It sailed past him and fell on the dusty snow.

Drat, thought Jack. He was going to have to think of something else. By now, Mr. Slick and his men had positioned themselves together as a trio, daring Jack to come their way.

Past them Jack saw an enormous hole in the ice. It must have been what Mr. Slick was looking at earlier. Figuring they'd caused it by that recent explosion, Jack had an idea of what to do next.

He pulled an oval-shaped plastic board out of his Book Bag. This was the GPF's Sno-Sled—the fastest way to slide in the snow. Sensing Jack was up to something, Mr. Slick and his men tried to protect themselves. Mr. Slick lifted his metal-tipped cane. One of his goons had that long tube; the other pulled out some sort of spiked ball on a rope.

But they weren't expecting what happened next. Jack picked up speed and sat in the middle of the Sno-Sled. As it accelerated, he held onto the handles.

Like a bowling ball, he crashed into the men's feet and sent them sailing backward into the hole in the ice.

SPLASH!

Jack and his Sno-Sled stopped short of the edge. Knowing the men could freeze in minutes, he had to get them out as fast as he could. He needed to rescue them, or he'd never figure out what the Black Arctic project was all about.

Giving the men his hand, he pulled them out one at a time. Just as he expected, Mr. Slick and his men were too cold to fight back. As he hauled them up onto the ice, Jack put some GPF handcuffs around their wrists. Then he put some foil blankets on the men to keep them warm.

Once he'd gotten them settled, Jack turned to Mr. Slick.

"Who are you working for?" he demanded.

Mr. Slick paused for a second then looked at Jack. Jack could tell in his eyes he was exhausted. After that dip in the frozen water, he looked like he'd aged at least ten years.

"Oh, what the heck, I'm getting too old for this stuff. Plus," he added, "I'm not getting paid enough. We were hired by Anton Gustavson."

Jack couldn't believe what he was hearing. Anton Gustavson was the president of the Wellem Oil and Gas Company.

"What did he want you to do?" asked Jack.

"Mr. Gustavson hired us to destroy the ice," Slick explained. "That way, he could access the oil easier, and use the Northwest Passage to ship it out."

Now Jack realized what the "black" meant in Black Arctic. The Arctic was seen by many as the last frontier when it came to precious oil. Billions of barrels' worth were thought to be trapped under the

Arctic sea. But drilling companies couldn't get to it easily if the ice was on the top and in the way. Blowing it up and melting it with that black tarp would make things easier. Plus, in accelerating the melt, the Northwest Passage (a normally frozen sea channel) would be available for ships to carry the oil out and sell it to the rest of the world. They had been attempting to speed up global warming for selfish, greedy needs—and Jack had stopped them in the nick of time.

Just then, Jack heard a comforting noise in the distance. It was the sound of several snowmobiles. The GPF backup troops had finally arrived.

Chapter 15:
The Director

One of the lead snowmobiles came up to
Jack. An adult driver got off and
introduced himself to Jack. He said his
name was Pablo and he worked for
Director Barter.

"Well," he said. "It looks like you've
solved another crime."

"Yep," said Jack. "These criminals are
ready for taking away. We also need to
arrest Mr. Anton Gustavson, since he's the

one who hired these men to destroy the ice."

"Why would he want to do that?" asked Pablo.

"Because he is a greedy man, who wants more oil," said Jack.

"What about the scientists?" Pablo said. "Are they all right?"

"They're OK now," said Jack. "They were just in the wrong place at the wrong time."

Jack gave Pablo the coordinates of the GPF Base Camp. He knew the scientists would be in good hands, and thanks to Jack would publish their findings as soon as they could.

"One more thing," said Jack. "We need to get rid of all this black tarp on the ice."

"Will do," said Pablo. "Director Barter is proud of you. He wants to speak to you now."

Pablo handed over a small videophone, and then stepped away. On the screen was a man with light skin and thick-rimmed specs. Jack was confused. This wasn't the man he'd met in the director's office.

"Great job, Secret Agent Courage," he said. "I knew you could do it."

"Thanks," said Jack. "So which one of you is the real director?"

"I'm afraid that's a secret that I can never reveal," the man said, before signing off with a smile.

Pablo came up to Jack. "I notice you aren't wearing your Watch Phone," he said.

"Yeah," said Jack, rubbing his wrist, "Mr. Slick broke it in two."

"Take this one," said Pablo, handing Jack a new Watch Phone.

As Jack thanked Pablo and strapped the watch onto his wrist, he looked over at Mr. Slick. His beaver teeth were still chattering, but he would survive. He and his men were about to be sent  to an international prison. Crimes this big against the environment affected all countries. Mr. Gustavson, Mr. Slick and his gang were definitely going away for a long time.

Once the commotion had died down, Jack tapped into his new Watch Phone. He called up a map of the world and pulled up the country of Great Britain.

There were no secrets among fellow GPF members. In front of everyone, he waited until a light shined brightly. When he was ready, he yelled "Off to England!"

Chapter 16:
The Last Word

When Jack arrived home the first thing he
did was head to his computer, sign on
and pull up his report on global warming.
Although he'd written most of it, there
was still some finishing up to do.

Tapping as furiously as he could, he
added:

*Many people think global warming
doesn't exist. Or, that if it does, it will only
give us sunnier weather. The truth is global*

warming is one of the biggest threats to humankind. Heating up the world, even by a few degrees, can change our weather and threaten everything that lives on Earth. Many animals, like the polar bear, may even die out in the next thirty years. That's why we have to do what we can to make a difference.

The single biggest thing that we can do is to cut down on the electricity we use. Most people don't know it, but electricity is made by burning coal. If we use less electricity, we burn less carbon dioxide. That means we should turn out the lights when we leave a room, and the power strips that run our computers. Another easy thing is to get our parents to change a light bulb.

If everyone in the country changed just one light bulb to one that says "CFL," it would be like taking one million cars off the road.

A normal household has at least fifteen to thirty light bulbs! Imagine if every kid nagged their parents to change them all; we really could save the world. Another thing we can do is use our bikes, skateboards and feet instead of cars to get around.

Global warming doesn't have to be scary. There are lots of villains out there who'd like it to succeed. But if we pull together, we can stop them and global warming altogether.

Jack pressed the "print" button and watched as his report came out. Exhausted from his trip, he switched the electrical power strip linked to his computer to "off" and changed into his pajamas. He crawled into bed and turned his nightlight off.

As he lay there letting his body sink into the mattress, he thought about the majesty of the Arctic. Knowing he'd rid that beautiful place of Mr. Slick and his goons made Jack smile with pride.

Tomorrow Jack would likely be off on another mission. He wondered where he was off to, and what kind of nasty villain he'd face. With dreams of exciting adventures ahead, Jack closed his eyes and drifted off to sleep.

About the Author

Elizabeth Singer Hunt is originally from Louisiana, and now lives in California. Inspired by her love of travel, she created the Jack Stalwart series for her children.

Find out more about
Secret Agent Jack Stalwart at

www.jackstalwart.com

Great games, puzzles,
free downloads,
activities, competitions
and much more!